McCREED'S
LAW

McCREED'S LAW

L. J. MARTIN

PINNACLE BOOKS
Kensington Publishing Corp.
http://www.kensingtonbooks.com

PINNACLE BOOKS are published by

Kensington Publishing Corp.
850 Third Avenue
New York, NY 10022

All Kensington Titles, Imprints, and Distributed Lines are avail-
able at special quantity discounts for bulk purchases for sales
promotions, premiums, fund-raising, and educational or insti-
tutional use. Special book excerpts or customized printings can
also be created to fit specific needs. For details, write or phone
the office of the Kensington special sales manager: Kensington
Publishing Corp., 850 Third Avenue, New York, NY 10022,
attn: Special Sales Department, Phone: 1-800-221-2647.

Pinnacle and the P logo Reg. U.S. Pat. & TM Off.

First Pinnacle Printing: June 2006

10 9 8 7 6 5 4 3 2 1

Printed in the United States of America

Chapter 1

"So, Flannigan, why haven't you called the Pinkertons? I hear they're doing right well after that cowardly killing of the James brothers' ma and little brother."

Morris Flannigan chomped down on his cigar and glared at redheaded Kane McCreed, but restrained himself. His tone was low, deliberate, and superior. "That firebombing killed Jesse James's half brother and only injured his mother. You need to get your facts right."

Flannigan reached over and flipped ash off his fat cigar into a spittoon next to his mahogany desk, resting near the end of the Transcontinental office railcar. Two green leather sofas flanked it on either side of the car, and a chest with mirrored doors was bolted to the wall, serving, Kane presumed, as a bar. Next to it, a small coal-fed fireplace with a grate front stood, also bracketed to the wall. It glowed, for even this late in March, the mornings in Cheyenne were white with frost. The car sat alone on a siding in the center of the Cheyenne, Wyoming, rail yard.

Flannigan sighed deeply. "McCreed, if this was a perfect world, we wouldn't have need of brindle-topped men like you for more than grubbin' out the privy. But it's not, and we occasionally do need the likes of you. So, you got a hankering for this ten-thousand-dollar reward, or not?"

Kane chuckled. "Least I got a full head of hair, Morris. So you've done tried the Pinkertons and they landed on their butt, as usual, as did the bluecoats?"

Again, Flannigan's tone was overly superior. "Pinkerton's men managed to catch you and your worthless brothers."

Kane hunkered forward, leaning his gnarled, slightly freckled knuckles on Flannigan's desk, and snarled, "The hell they did, boyo. Red Murphy and a bunch of rock hard trailsmen from Bozeman rode us down. The Pinkertons were five miles behind, eating Red's dust. Gerrad and Killian and I were trading off on one damn-near-dead rank broomtail, after Red sneaked up Dead Woman Canyon and shot our horses where they were tied at the cabin rail. A damn cowardly act, if you ask me." Kane continued to rest his knuckles on the desk and lean forward ominously. "And don't speak of my brothers, or I'll feed you that cigar, hot end first, understand?"

Flannigan shrugged, but sat back out of Kane's easy reach.

Kane curled his lip at him. "Even a fat man filling a city suit the size of your'n could have caught up—"

Flannigan reddened. "Fat or not, you're the old boy did time."

"And you lost a flea-bitten boat, which wouldn't have happened had you paid your debts to three fellas trying to get by chopping wood for your lousy steamships. But the Union Pacific is not famous for keeping their word." Kane's tone changed, and he guffawed. "You should have seen that little brass whistle sticking up out of the water, Flannigan. I hear she still parks her broad butt on the bottom of the Missouri, where I'd put this whole damn railroad, had I my choice."

Flannigan sat back in his reclining chair. "And if you hadn't had debts owed you from half the damn jury in Helena, you'd still be rotting in the bottom of Deer Lodge Prison." Now it was Flannigan's turn to chuckle, and he shook his head. "You want a shot or not?"

"Put it in writing."

Flannigan, sitting forward, again reddened. "Hell, man, there're posters all over the territory—"

"In writing, addressed to me personal, and signed by Lawrence Hawthorn, his highfalutin, fat, bald self."

"Hawthorn is a busy man, Kane. He leaves this minor business up to me. Railroad security is my—"

"In writing, signed by Hawthorn, in my hand before I fork my buckskin and ride after that hell-on-the-hoof half-breed. I'll cool my heels in Cheyenne for a week; then I'm heading back to Montana, and you and the railroad can chugalug off to hell."

"All right, all right. Damn the flies! I'll telegram him today. You'll have your letter of agreement in three days, if he can get to it."

"And five hundred dollars in advance for expenses."

Flannigan bit down on the cigar so hard it vibrated, dropping ash on his desk. "Don't press your luck, McCreed."

"In gold, not lousy railroad script." Kane reached in to a wooden cuspidor on the desk and gathered up a half dozen of the fat cigars, stuffed them in his linsey-woolsey shirt pocket, spun on his booted heel, and headed for the doorway at the rear of the car.

Flannigan stammered, "I'll hand you the coin when I get the authorization from Hawthorn, less five dollars for my damn cigars."

"Fine," Kane called over his shoulder. "I've got drinkin' money to last me a few days. This is Friday. Next Thursday, I ride out . . . north to heaven and home or nor'west to hell and Chaco's hidey-hole, it's up to you."

Flannigan waited for the door to slam before he muttered, "You son of a bitch. I wish you would have hanged." But he walked to the car window and slid it down, then yelled to Kane, who was jumping the tracks heading for the row of saloons and brothels along Campstool Road.

"Kane, bring me Chaco's head! On a platter, and you'll get your ten thousand!"

Kane merely waved over his shoulder.

Flannigan yelled even louder.

"Kane . . . bring me Chaco's head!"

Then he slammed the window upward so hard it cracked.

"Damn the flies," he muttered, then retook his desk chair to write the telegram to the president of the Union Pacific. Hawthorn wouldn't be happy, but he'd send the letter. Chaco Sixdog was becoming a deep, expensive thorn in the side of the railroad, and Kane McCreed knew both Chaco and the country.

And Kane McCreed was probably the only man in the territory who could ride him down. Even the damned Army had been unsuccessful.

It would be a snapping wolverine after a den of bloodthirsty wolves.

Daisy Dunnigan's Parlor and Ladies' Rooming House had a fine cypress bar to which two dozen men could belly up, and a polished cypress back bar with a mirror as wide as a man was tall. Over the mirror hung a painting of a finely endowed French lady in full recline, with considerably less than full attire.

Kane admired the painting as he waited while a mustached bartender, whose red-veined nose testified to his sampling his own product, poured him three fingers of fine Tullumore Dew Irish Whiskey. But his mind was on the task at hand.

What Morris Flannigan and the Union Pacific didn't know was that Kane, hopefully with the help of his kin, would go after Chaco Sixdog had they had to pay the U.P. to do so. Sixdog and his band of half-breeds had robbed the train, killing a dozen passengers and crew, while it was in a long slow climb up the steepest part of South Pass. They'd gotten away with not only several thousand in government money, but with a half-dozen surviving passengers. Passengers Kane knew were the pick of the litter; passengers who looked as if they'd bring high ransom.

One of those passengers was Vivian Flynn, whose husband had been killed in the ensuing gun battle.

Shamus Flynn, formerly a city marshal in Dodge City, was an old friend of Kane's; a friend who had won Vivian's hand in marriage. Kane had stood up with them in Cairo, Illinois, just after the war, even though it knotted his gut to do so. He'd never told Vivian or Shamus, but his heart, hard as it was, was Vivian's, and had long been so. She was a beautiful woman, one who didn't know how beautiful she was. And she was prettier on the inside than the out—a true Irish lass, with surprising Nordic beauty—the spawn of Viking invaders centuries before, with blond hair and gray-green eyes.

Kane's heart had withered that day, the day Shamus and Vivian had married, although he'd never let on to her or his friend.

The fact Chaco Sixdog had her gnawed at Kane's backbone like a dog worrying a beef-bone. Kane meant to get her back and again put her safely on her way to San Francisco, if that was what she wished.

Getting paid for the task was merely a bonus.

But it was a bonus that would buy him a two-thousand-acre cattle spread, backing up to a million acres of free-graze federal land. A spread he'd long admired up near Big Horn City where the Yellowstone and the Big Horn met up; one that would put him on his way to an honest life.

He'd acted casual in front of Flannigan, but the fact was, he was chewing at the bit to be after Chaco. Hanging around, waiting for the expense money and the letter of agreement, would drive him loony, but it was necessary. It had already been almost a month since Chaco had robbed the train, and there'd been no ransom demands; but they would come. Chaco had already learned the value of white women, by selling them back twice before. But this time he'd picked a rich target—the Union Pacific. The delay had already given Chaco and his men time to get well into the mountains, probably the Big Horns or on over in the Absarokas, and time to relax and believe that no one would find them. Chaco was as clever as a wounded grizzly when someone was on his tail.

The fact was, Kane had a good idea where he'd be holed up. They had shared a cell at Deer Lodge for the better part of a year, and although they'd not been friends, you couldn't be housed with seven other men and not learn something, overhear something, about each of them. And for a half-Indian, Chaco was a talker.

Kane had remade one real good friend while in prison. Toby Andrews had ridden with the 60th Infantry Illinois Volunteers mustered at Camp Dubois, Anna, Illinois, and was doing two years for shooting up some fellas with whom he'd had a claim dispute. Although Kane and Toby hadn't known each other well until late in the war, they'd rectified that under fire. They'd fought, nearly shoulder to shoulder, in Murfreesboro, Chattanooga, Buzzard Roost, Ringgold, Dalton, and on and on until Averyboro, where the regiment was completely surrounded and Toby and his company had fought their way through enemy lines. Kane and Toby Andrews had often fought side by side, hand to hand with the Rebs, and that would bring any man close to his brother in arms, even if he couldn't call him by name.

Kane had been glad to see him, but would have preferred better circumstances.

But one cold moonless night Chaco Sixdog had murdered Toby Andrews in his sleep, making sure that every man in the cell knew who did it. Kane had been clubbed down by the guards for trying to beat Chaco to death. He learned when he got out of the hole, six months later, that Chaco had escaped during his trial for the murder of Toby Andrews.

The word got back to Kane that Chaco had killed Toby for only one reason, so he'd be brought to trial on the outside, where his band of outlaws could break him out of a local lockup.

It had worked, but he'd left a bad enemy behind. Kane meant to get him, and, now that he'd kidnapped Vivian, would ride until his horse fell under him, then hike until he died himself, but he wouldn't quit until he had Chaco's hide to use for butt-wipe.

As he sipped his whiskey, it was all he could do not to go ahead and, ride out without the letter of agreement from the Union Pacific, but he needed the seed money. It was a hell of a ride into the Big Horns, and even more if it took him to the Absarokas, and he wanted a pair of saddle-scabbard guns and a pair of sidearms, not to speak of a couple of pack mules, a spare horse, and two months' worth of grub.

No, he would wait. He owed it to Toby and to Vivian, and to his old friend Shamus, to ride Chaco down and bleed him out a drop at a time.

A blond barmaid in a low-cut Kelly-green-and-black lace-trimmed gown sidled up to him, taking his thoughts away from his coming quest.

"You lookin' to buy a girl a drink, laddy?" the sandy-haired soiled dove asked him as she laid a gentle hand on his shoulder.

"I'd be happy to stand you to a drink, lass, but it would be for here, not for upstairs. A fella in my frame of mind would be poor company."

She laughed. "Oh, come on, Red, it's not your frame of mind I'd be interested in. But I . . . Say, bucko, wouldn't you be one of the McCreed clan? You're stubby enough, redheaded enough, and an ax-handle wide through the shoulders, and have a way about you. . . ."

Chapter 2

He eyed her with keen interest. "And what would you be knowing of the McCreeds?"

"Why, boyo, young Kill McCreed and I were tight as ticks in a lamb's tail. I gave him a wee touch of heaven more than once, right up those stairs."

Kane laughed aloud. Then offered, "Killian would be the last whelp of our litter."

"You wait right here." She spun on her heel and headed for the stairway.

In moments, as the bartender was pouring Kane his second, she came back down the stairs, followed by a lady Kane had known well as a wet-behind-the-ears youth back in Illinois. Daisy Collingsworth, a little heavier, a few crow's-feet at the corners of her eyes, but still a fine-looking woman—a neighbor from a farm not far from his father's worked-out sand heap.

He spread his arms wide, and she ran into them for a heels-in-the-air hug.

"My God, Daisy, how long has it been?" Kane asked, placing her back on her feet.

"Since you went away to that damnable war," she

said, pushing away and eyeing him up and down. "Jesus and Mother Mary, you've grown into one hell of a bucko. You ain't the tallest tree in the woods, but you look to be here to stay. Fact is, right now, you're as pretty as a Wyoming sunset."

"I've been called a lot of things in my time, but never pretty. But you're a beautiful woman, Daisy Collingsworth . . . or is it Daisy Dunnigan?"

She turned to the barmaid before she answered. "You got customers across the room, Wilma. . . ."

"Yes, ma'am," the girl said, and swished away to a table full of cowhands playing poker. The place was beginning to fill with townsmen, railroad workers, and hands from the nearby farms and ranches. The noise was up a notch, as men played poker, faro, and at a wheel of chance.

"Yes, this is my joint, such as it is," Daisy said, "And I go by Dunnigan, not that I came by it honestly. I spent some . . . some communal time . . . with Myron Dunnigan, who built this establishment, first as a false-front and tent-back hellhole when this was nothing more than a hell-on-wheels railroad town, and soon, for propriety's sake, Myron took to introducing me as Mrs. Dunnigan." She moved closer and lowered her voice so no one could overhear. "We wasn't married, except in the eyes of the Lord, but no one knew that when he got shot down out in the street. I took over the place as if it was rightfully mine, and got no argument . . . so here I am. But tell me about you, Kane. I saw your little brother not too many months ago, and told him to send you my way should he stumble across your ugly hide."

"You come a long ways from an Illinois milkmaid, Daisy. As to Killian," Kane lied, "I haven't seen him. I came here for a job of work, and just wandered in off the street."

"And your older brother, Gerrad?"

"He's out on the Pacific somewhere, maybe Alaska, last I heard."

"By all that's holy, I'm loving the Lord for sending you my way, among other of his blessings. Now, about you? You cuttin' a fat hog?"

"Like most everybody out West, it's been a hard row to hoe, but I'm not complaining. As Kill may have mentioned, he, Gerrad, and I spent a little time in the Montana State Prison for a misunderstanding with the railroad—"

"I heard you sunk a side-wheeler, owned by the road, 'cause they didn't pay up. Just like you to pick on the little fella."

"—and we ended up with the short end of the stick."

"Not surprised. Most do who tangle with the road. So, what's brother Gerrad doing at sea?"

"He's an independent sort, as you might remember . . . probably not, as you were no taller than a goose, Gerrad sailed off around the world before I really got to know him, till he caught up with us in Montana, just in time to get caught up in the side-wheeler thing. I got to know him real well in Deer Lodge Prison, but he headed out for Seattle and the sea as soon as we got out. He said he didn't want to see any stone walls for the rest of his days.

"I was only five when he left, climbed on a riverboat and headed down the Chicago River. He left Illinois on an ore boat up through Lake Michigan, down Lake Huron, up Lake Erie, then east through the Erie Canal. That was the last I heard of him for over twenty years, till he looked us up in Helena.

"Anyway, it seems I'm about to mend that fence, as I'm off to do a chore for Flannigan."

Her face fell. "Flannigan doesn't hire men unless it's them, rather than him, he'd care to see in harm's way."

Kane smiled tightly. "It seems one's got to go down the hard road to end up living easy. I'll find my gold one way or the other."

"Or lead," Daisy said, still not smiling. "So, what's this chore?"

"Chaco Sixdog."

She stared at him for a minute, then said, "I'd like to see his eyes being picked by the crows as he hangs from the railroad water tower, but don't do it, Kane. He's a devil, not a man. He killed four men right here in this saloon three years ago, two shot dead, two cut from ear to ear with that brush cutter he wears as a belt knife. It was a chore that made him grin like the only two-dollar whore in a gold-strike town."

"It's a done thing, Daisy. I'm off as soon as I get a letter from the road and a little money."

"If it's a stake you're needing, I'll be happy—"

He hushed her with a shake of the head.

She waved the bartender over. "Sam, give my late-departed friend here a drink. Anything he wants, as it's damn near his last."

As the bartender was pouring another Tullumore Dew, she gave Kane another hug, then pushed away. "I'm going back to my bookwork. I've lost too many fine friends over the years to fall in love with another, even if it's only an old-friend kind of love. You need anything, you send Wilma up to fetch me."

"Good to see you, Daisy."

"I'll pray I see you again, Kane." With that, she spun on her heel and headed back up the stairway.

She'd no more than topped the stairs when Kane, eyeing the mirror across the bar, saw a tall man stop behind him. "McCreed," the man said, and his tone wasn't friendly.

Kane turned slowly. The man, in a city suit and narrow-brimmed hat, was a half head taller than him, but not nearly so thick through chest and shoulders. He looked trim and fast, but one who wouldn't finish the race if it was for endurance. He wore a short chin beard, pork-chop sideburns, and a cocky look. Kane noted the beard was to cover a receding chin and a protruding Bulldog Colt on his hip.

"And who's asking?" Kane asked, but was fairly sure he knew, as the man wore a copper badge on his waist-coat.

"Obviously I know who you are. I'm Collin Gratsworth, city marshal of Cheyenne. You know where I might find one Killian McCreed? Rejoyeth in the truth, and you will be among the chosen."

"And why would you be looking for me little brother?"

"It's retribution time. He near beat two of my deputies to death out in the alley behind the livery across the tracks not long after he got out of my jail for being drunk and disturbing the peace—"

"If he did, they prodded him a while."

"—and I've got a warrant for him for assault. He's a wanted man. One of those men still has a crooked arm. This is a God-fearing town, and it's an eye for an eye—"

"Haven't seen old Kill in a month of Sundays."

"And wouldn't tell me if you had. A Christian man would."

Kane didn't bother to respond to that, just gave him a

smile with one side of his mouth, then turned back to his drink.

"I'm not finished," Gratsworth said.

Kane, his back to the man, spoke to him in the mirror. "You a preacher, or a town marshal? Don't matter. Seems your business is with Killian, not Kane Mc-Creed. Take it to him and let me drink in peace."

Gratsworth grabbed Kane by the shoulder, and spun him back around; at the same time, two other men with badges stepped up closer behind the marshal. Both of them looked as if they'd at one time loaded drays for a living, built more like Kane than the marshal. One carried an ugly scar from a nipped-off ear down his neck to his collar; the other had a sling on his arm and should be little trouble . . . of course, it wasn't his gun arm, judging by the revolver on his hip.

"You—" the marshal started to say.

But Kane interrupted. "That would be my best shirt you tugged on, Marshal."

Gratsworth poked the long index finger of his left hand hard into Kane's breastbone, at the same time resting his right hand on the butt of the Bulldog. "By Jehovah, no man turns his back on me," he snarled.

Quick as a praying mantis on a fly, Kane grasped Gratsworth's pointing finger with his right and locked his left on Gratsworth's wrist, so he couldn't pull the weapon.

He wrenched the finger hard. Gratsworth screamed and went to his knees, managing to free the Bulldog as he slunk down. Kane cracked the man's gun hand on the bar as he sagged, and the Bulldog spun over the bar and to the floor on the working side.

Both deputies took a quick step forward, but Kane stopped them, wrenching the finger even harder and making Gratsworth scream like a turpentined cat leading a pack of dogs.

"Stop where you stand," Kane snapped, "or I'll hand you his ugly finger for the pickle jar."

Deputy Marcus McMann and Deputy Hiram Lavender stopped, but both stepped back to pull weapons from hip holsters.

Kane smiled, released the finger, grabbed the marshal by his lapels, and dragged him up to his feet. Kane released him when he was on his feet—wavering, but standing—smoothed the suit coat as the marshal stood half in shock, rubbing his finger, his mouth hanging open.

Kane smiled at him as he spoke. "You dropped your gun over the bar, laddy." He turned to the bartender. "Kind sir, would you be fetching the marshal's stubby little gun?"

Before he could turn back, all three of them fell on him, the deputies swinging their weapons as bludgeons. With his back to the bar, he gave as good as he got, until they all backed away, one of the deputies bleeding badly from the nose, the other holding a hand to a split eyebrow as blood wept through his fingers. The marshal had been knocked reeling to the floor, but was again on his feet. The three of them had weapons leveled on him. Kane had never reached for his English-made Bland-Pryce revolver, still strapped down in his holster; he wasn't about to draw on the law, unless he knew they were shooting.

"Not only will the Good Lord smite you for your sins . . . but you're under arrest," Gratsworth said as he spit, wiping blood from his mouth.

"Collin!" The clear sound of a woman's voice came from halfway up the stairway. Daisy Dunnigan stood with a sawed-off scattergun in hand, both barrels cocked and leveled at Gratsworth's midsection.

"I'm arresting this man," Gratsworth managed, but his voice was weak.

"That's city business, maybe. But as I've pointed out more'n once to you and those louts you bunch of town hypocrites call deputies, Dunnigan's is not in the city. Go file a complaint with the county sheriff . . . or the Good Lord above . . . so we can tell them him how you assaulted one of my customers who was merely minding his own business having a quiet drink. Marcus . . . Hiram . . . that goes for all of you.

"As I recall, there's no love lost between any of you and one of my better customers . . . Sheriff Harrigan. And, Collin, I'd bet your dollar against one of my two dollar tokens, there is no love lost between you and the Lord God . . . no matter how much you blather his good name about." She paused as Gratsworth clamped his jaw but did not respond, so she continued. "You've got no call to come into my place and harass my customers. Do what you have to do, Collin, but do it in the city. Now, get along with you and let us be."

Gratsworth stared long and hard at Daisy and the scattergun. "You'll pay for this, Miss Daisy. Pay hard and heavy. This is a house of sin and you're a jezebel—"

"And," Daisy said with a wide grin, "you've sinned here aplenty. From now on, it's gonna take you two tokens to everyone else's one."

Kane couldn't contain his smile as he sucked a deep breath and mopped a bloody forehead with one of the towels that hung under the bar at four-foot intervals. He'd caught the butt of a heavy revolver, and the color was some deeper red than his hair. He turned back to the bar, again giving his back to the marshal. The bartender had fetched the Bulldog and was handing it to Kane. He took it by the barrel, turned, then casually handed it to Gratsworth. "Don't be cocking that, Daisy might get me with the overspray. Can I buy you a drink, Marshal?" Kane asked, but his grin said he was less than sincere.

Gratsworth's eyes narrowed. "Demon rum . . . " he started to say, them thought better of it, and his voice lowered. "You bet, McCreed. Let's go into town where the whiskey's not watered down."

"I believe I'd prefer to do my drinking right here, if it's all the same."

"It ain't. Let's go," Gratsworth commanded his men, and they followed him out. "See you in church, Daisy," he called over his shoulder as he pushed through the door. He paused halfway out, turned back, and glowered at Kane. "And I'll see you're in hell, along with your worthless kin." Then he slammed the door so hard its glass panels vibrated.

Daisy walked on down the stairs, handed the scatter-gun to the bartender, and sidled up next to Kane.

"You always was trouble on the hoof," she said, then turned to Sam, the bartender. "Sam, I believe I'll be joining Mr. McCreed with a wee dollop of that sweet dew of the Irish bogs."

"Thank you," Kane said sincerely. "How-some-ever, you should know I didn't ask for that little run-in with that . . . how did you say it . . . that blatherin' fool."

Daisy laughed. "You know, you could have just answered the man's questions. Don't try politics, Kane. It ain't your long suit."

Kane raised his glass to her. "Questions is one thing. Laying on of hands is another." Then he smiled. "To you, Mrs. Dunnigan, and to stretching Sixdog's neck."

She returned the smile and toasted back. "May your

eyes be the first to glisten with happy tears, may your strength be strong enough to chase off your fears. Be the victor, not victim, be a star or a clod, but mostly be Irish in love with Lord God." She smiled, and touched his glass with hers. "When the time comes, and God forbid it be soon, may you be in heaven a full hour afore the devil, or Gratsworth and his hypocrite kind, know you're dead."

He laughed. "I'll live long enough to pour a bottle of good whiskey on Gratsworth's grave . . . of course, I'll process it first." They laughed, and drank.

"Don't be going into town," she cautioned, after downing the drink and waving at Sam for another for both of them.

Kane dug into a pocket, but this time it was Daisy who put a finger in his chest. "Hey, bucko, it's my whiskey I'm pouring here, and you're a guest in my house."

"I can pay my way, Daisy."

"Tomorrow. Tonight, it's for old times."

"Old times," he toasted again, and they upended the glasses.

"May they not be the best times," Daisy added, and slammed her glass on the bar for another. Then she gave him a coy smile, and added, "May the best times be yet to come."

Chapter 3

Chaco Sixdog sat easily in a Crow saddle on a long-legged paint stallion, watching the stage station in the deep canyon below. The stage road from Virginia City, Montana, to Rockville, Wyoming, wound through this rock canyon in the Wind River Mountains, not but a day's ride from where they'd laired up in a deep, expansive cave in a canyon below rugged rocks, including some that rose high and narrow, known as needles. Normally, he'd be watching the station to see what he could steal, but that was not his intent.

Beside him, on a tall sorrel, carrying a McClellan saddle, sat an older man in buckskins. Where Sixdog's hair was long, braided, relatively clean, and coal black, his accomplice's was gray, matted, filthy, and only shoulder-length. Sixdog's wide face was pocked deeply from a run-in with the white man's smallpox when a youth. His deep-set eyes seemed to miss nothing.

The other man hadn't shaved in months, and being a white man—barely discernible as he hadn't bathed in the same period—his beard grew long and thick.

"Only the fresh team, a six-up, four mules and two

wheelhorses . . . half-Clydesdale by the size of 'em . . . and a couple of saddle horses in the corral," the older man said. "Only the station keeper and his wife in residence, I'd wager."

"We wait," Sixdog said. "No moon tonight. Dark soon." The other man didn't argue. He'd learned long ago, if you rode with Sixdog, you didn't argue.

"Let's tie these nags in the brush and get some rest. I got a jug of corn."

"You always have jug of corn, Teacher. Stay sober till after. You can drink till you see your ghosts on the ride back."

Chaco didn't call the older man Teacher out of respect, but because it was what he called himself. Before he'd become such a good friend of John Barleycorn, and sunk to the low depths of riding with a band of half-breeds and cutthroats, he'd been a teacher. But whiskey had brought him down, and far more whiskey after he'd lost his position had brought him hand in hand with the devil. Nothing was beneath him, if it meant he could get his whiskey. His nose was bulbous and veined with the badge of a hard-drinking man, and his pale eyes watered in the wind and sun over cheeks almost constantly burned red. He'd taken to chewing tobacco, and it stained his gray beard in streaks.

"I'll only drink a smidgen," he said, dismounting and leading the horse away from the edge. Chaco eyed him coldly, but said nothing. He needed the man, to write the white man's scratching and to interpret his more difficult spoken words. There would come a day when he'd be fed up with the drunken old man and would slit his gullet, but not this day.

He too dismounted, and followed the old man into the brush where they could not be seen from the road below.

The old man dug a jug out of his saddlebags, and Chaco snatched it out of his hands, unstoppered it, and took a long draw. He needed a drink if he was going to have to put up with Teacher's drinking.

Dark covered the land, and the moon was lazy this night and not yet in the sky, when they tightened the cinches and began to let the horses pick their way down the steep slope.

Chaco dismounted a hundred yards from where a light glowed in the cabin window. The thick plank door would never be opened to an Indian, particularly after dark, so Teacher continued and reined up forty feet opposite the front door. Rather than dismount, he sat the horse as he called out.

"Hello the house! Can you accommodate a tired stranger?"

He could see a finger of light as something was removed from covering a peephole in the door; then the light went away, as he presumed an eye covered the tiny opening; then a voice rang out. "Come up on the porch so I can see you."

Teacher reined the sorrel over to a hitching rail, dismounted, tied him, but this time, didn't bother to loosen the cinch. A fast getaway could still be in order.

He stomped up onto the porch, brushed off his buckskins, then eyed the peephole. "I'd trade a pull or two on a bottle of good corn for a bowl of beans."

"Hunger is the curse of the indolent, and often of those who partake an excess of demon rum," the voice said.

"Blessed are they which do hunger and thirst after righteousness: for they shall be filled. Matthew 6:5," Teacher said, his voice ringing with reverence.

"A man who knows and loves the Bible is welcome here anytime," the voice said.

Teacher heard a heavy bar being removed from the door. It opened, and a man his own age but with well-trimmed hair and clean clothes, with reading glasses perched on his nose, stood with a single-barrel shotgun in hand, but hanging loosely at his side. "Where you from, friend, and where you headed?" he asked, his voice friendly enough.

"Come over from the Green River country. Been hunting beaver and wolves for hides, but they're scarce as hen's teeth. Headed north to the Judith Country to keep after the wolf."

"Leave your weapons on your animal, and come on in."

Teacher moved back to the animal, put his belt knife and revolver in the saddlebag, at the same time fishing out the jug of corn. He returned to the step, then lifted his arms to show he carried no weapons and did a pirouette like a toy ballet dancer atop a music box. He smiled broadly, showing tobacco-stained teeth, and waited for the man to step aside.

"Martha, put the stew pot back on the fire. We got us a visitor." The man looked over his shoulder, then stepped aside to let Teacher enter.

"Obliged," Teacher said, watching closely as the man returned the shotgun to a rack over the front door made from a pair of pronghorn antelope horns.

When done, he eyed Teacher with little enthusiasm, but he extended his hand. "I'm Clarence Pettibone, and that's my wife Martha."

"Pleased," Teacher said, giving the hand a pump. "Oscar Brown," he said, lying.

A pudgy nondescript woman with a lace-trimmed dust cap over mouse-brown hair, in a loose-fitting gingham dress, stood at the stove, feeding it a few sticks. She glanced up long enough to nod, then went back to her chores.

"Take a seat and my woman will pour you some coffee."

The long table in the center of the room would seat a dozen, and looked out of place jammed in as it was. A variety of chairs surrounded the table, most of them ladderback, a couple of them with turned stiles, one fancy one with an upholstered seat and wheat-leaf splat, two without backs at all that were no more than stools. Teacher knew this was to accommodate stage line passengers. He presumed the only other door led to the couple's sleeping quarters. He took the seat nearest the front door.

"This would be a stage station?" Teacher asked, eyeing the table.

"It would. Stage runs from the Union Pacific down at Rockville up to Virginia City, Montana. They be more'n a dozen stops along the way. Ever' third day, I got to have a fresh team ready. The pull up out of here south is one of the worst on the line, so we generally run four mules and two wheel horses."

"And the stage up-line and down-line sends them back three days later?"

"That's how it works. Going north, then three days later going south. Several new strikes up Montana way, so we generally got a full load of folks, and we got the mail contract."

Teacher took one sip of the cup of coffee the woman set in front of him. "Smells larrupin' good," he said as she returned to stir the stew.

He took a sip, yawned wide, then stood. "Ma'am,

you'll pardon me, but I got to use the necessary." He pointed at the door and asked Mr. Pettibone, "Out back?"

Pettibone nodded, and took a seat halfway down the table. "I'd have another cup, Martha," he said, and she frowned at him.

"You don't sleep well when you overdo."

"One more, Martha," he grumbled, and she sighed, as Teacher moved on outside. He stood by the door, and listened to make sure the man had not replaced the bar.

He coughed deeply, a prearranged signal, and Chaco appeared from around the corner. He moved silently on moccasined feet, staying close to the wall so he couldn't be seen through the peephole.

Teacher extended an upraised finger, indicating he wanted to wait for a bit, then moved to the door, swung it aside, and stepped in. Pettibone still sat at the table sipping coffee, and the missus stood at the stove, stirring her stew.

"You best fill another bowl," Teacher said, and Chaco's broad body filled the doorway; in each hand he held a revolver, but they hung loosely.

Mrs. Pettibone gasped, but Clarence merely glared. "You riding with the likes of him?" he asked Teacher.

"I am. Unless you're the circuit judge hereabouts, and are ready to pass judgment on me, keep your mouth shut and maybe he won't dissect your liver."

"He fashions evil for himself who does evil to another," Pettibone said, "and an evil plan does mischief to the planner."

"I don't believe I know that one," Teacher said, then added, "Of course, Plato said, 'No evil can happen to a good man, either in life or after death.' I would suggest you and the missus act right good while we visit a spell."

"I believe, sir," Pettibone said, slightly red in the face

from being deceived by a man who quoted the Bible, "that you're a sanctimonious son of a bitch."

Teacher took a menacing step forward. "And if I were the man looking at two fellas who'd as soon ventilate his hide, I'd watch the waggle of my tongue."

"I just cannot abide a man who'd quote the Bible, then do mischief."

"Clarence," Martha snapped, entering the exchange for the first time, "we've had a long good life, and I'd as soon not end it at just this moment. You're the one being sanctimonious at the moment, and for the sake of your dear departed mother, I won't add the last part. Let's just listen to what these gentlemen have to say while I ladle up some stew."

They both took a seat, and Chaco set a revolver on the table on either side of his place setting.

Teacher took a long draw on the jug, then set it down in front of himself. "I'd share this, but it seems I don't have to now." He flashed tobacco-stained teeth at Pettibone, who didn't bother to reply.

The woman served the stew to them, along with a chunk of fine oven-fresh bread. They ate in silence, until Pettibone, staring at Chaco, finally asked, "You Shoshone?"

Chaco gave him a glance that would peel paint off the walls, had the walls been painted, but nodded. "The good half. The man who raped my mother was Irish scum." He finished the stew, waved at the woman and grunted, and she carried the pot over and poured the last of it in his bowl. Teacher drank peacefully, his eyes only half open, until Chaco finished.

"Give him the paper," Chaco said to Teacher, who snapped awake.

Teacher dug into his shirt and came up with a folded

piece of foolscap. He handed it to the stationmaster, who opened it on the table in front of him and read it carefully, then glanced up, his eyes a little wide.

"You Chaco Sixdog?"

The closest Chaco normally came to a smile was a curled lip. He raised it in Pettibone's direction, then answered, "You want me rape your ugly woman and slit your gullet to prove?"

Anger flashed in Pettibone's eyes, but he contained himself, then said levelly, "No, sir. Just leave us in peace with your stomach full of Martha's good cooking and with our blessing."

"Don't need blessing," Chaco muttered. Then he reached across the table and took the jug out of Teacher's grasp and took a long pull, but his eyes never left Pettibone.

"What do I do with this?" Pettibone asked, holding up the paper. "I sure ain't got no two thousand dollars times six."

Teacher gave him another tobacco-stained smile. "Put it on the stage south—"

"Be here tomorrow."

"Good. Put it on the stage, get it to the powers who be at the railroad." Teacher stood. "Thanks for the grub. A pleasure not to have to kill you."

"My pleasure," Pettibone said, and Teacher almost admired him for a moment, maintaining a smidgen of a sense of humor under the circumstance.

"Like it says in that paper," Teacher said, working up the meanest look he could muster, "they don't get us the money, you'll start getting pieces and parts of hostages. Understand?"

"Yes, sir," Pettibone said, and Martha looked as if she was going to be sick.

Chaco headed for the door, with Teacher at his heels. Teacher paused in the doorway, and eyed the two of them. "That was a fine stew, ma'am. Don't fail us, Clarence, or it'll be pure ol' hell to pay . . . pardon me, ma'am. And don't open this door till we've had time to clear out, or the missus will be digging lead out of your hide."

Clarence nodded, and the door slammed.

When both of them were full of Tullumore Dew up to the gills, Kane was invited up to Daisy's personal quarters, which were much nicer than he imagined. She enjoyed a sitting room, with a small second-story privy, which fell into a ditch dug from upstream on Crow Creek and ran right up against the rear of the establishment, then back to the creek. Her personal bedroom was the size of the sitting room, and a covered porch ran all across the back of the building, with a bed that folded down, where one could sleep with a view of the stars and hills and mountains beyond.

Kane was relegated to the porch, somewhat to his surprise, considering the business of the establishment.

He spent the next three days busying himself with chores about the place in payment for his room and board. Daisy, who seldom cooked, but was excellent in the kitchen, returned to it while this friend from Illinois was in residence. Her Irish soda bread and colcannon— mashed potatoes with chopped-up cabbage—reminded Kane of his ma's cooking.

On the morning of the fourth day, he was summoned back to the Union Pacific office car, still parked on a siding within sight of Daisy's.

He climbed up onto the landing, and entered. Flannigan

was again alone, sitting at his desk. Without bothering with hello, Kane asked, "You got my letter and money?"

Flannigan looked up and eyed him distastefully. "I got a letter that you might be interested in."

"Oh."

Flannigan unfolded a piece of worn foolscap and began to read. "We have, still in good health, Mr. Alexander Potts, his wife and child; Mrs. Vivian Flynn, Mrs. Marybeth Pettersen, and Mrs. Angela Bolander. They will stay in good health, should you forthwith deliver the sum of two thousand dollars per head, in gold coin, to the Greybull Canyon stage stop. No later than April 15th, or we will begin a systematic execution of the hostages. Their blood will be on the railroad's hands."

Chapter 4

Flannigan threw the paper down on his desk.

"Is it signed?" Kane asked.

"With an X, but someone printed his name below. Chaco Sixdog."

"Chaco didn't write this note," Kane said.

"Of course he didn't, he's a stupid savage."

"Ignorant in civilized ways maybe, stupid, no. He's a combination of fox, badger, and cougar in the woods. So, what is the railroad gonna do?"

"See that pile on my desk? That's telegrams from St. Louis. Seems this Potts fella was well known and liked there. They're sending letters to Washington by the wagonful and threatening to sue the railroad and worse, to send out their own posse to run Sixdog down. And some farmer up in Wisconsin is on his way here to go it alone to find his wife—Marybeth is her name. All we need is a bunch of Missouri city boys raising dust all over the hills until Sixdog fills their hides with lead. There are a half-dozen reporters camped out in town, badgering me every day about what we're doing to get these folks back and sending telegrams to their papers telling half the country what a bunch of louts we are." Flannigan sighed deeply. "We're going to pay up. We can't have folks not riding the trains because they think the railroad will let something like this happen and not do anything about it."

"So," Kane said with a snarl, "where's my letter and money, so I can get on the road and maybe save you louts some money?"

"Hawthorn is hunting with some visiting English nobleman, somewhere in the Black Hills. He can't be reached and isn't due back for more'n a week."

"I've got to leave now if I'm going to find hostages in time to get them the hell out before the blood runs."

Flannigan rose and walked to stare out one of the train car windows. "Hell, McCreed, it's a damn folly to think you might pull this off. I'm going to recommend that we pay the ransom and let the Army handle it."

"Then you're gonna go back on our agreement?" Kane said, his voice low and a little ominous.

Flannigan turned and looked a little apprehensive. "I told you, it had to come from Omaha. You can't handle this alone. Hell, there's no telling how many of them are riding with Chaco."

"Who said I was riding alone?"

"I sure ain't seen no sign of cohorts."

"You may not be lookin' in the right place. How much can you advance, without hearing from Hawthorn?"

"I can come up with the five hundred, if you'll take the existence of the posters as guarantee that you'll be paid the rest on delivery."

"No problem, Flannigan, since I don't have time to wait. But you tell Hawthorn that my stinking one little ol' side-wheeler is a sniper with a slingshot compared to a barrage of cannon, should he fail to pay up."

"I can't advance money to someone who's threatening the railroad, McCreed. You ain't much of a politician."

"That's the second time I've heard that in almost as many days. And it don't bother me much. You know how to tell if a politician is lying?"

"No, how?"

"If his pie hole is flappin'. So calling me 'not much of one' is a fine compliment." He smiled, then the smile faded. "You want to save yourself a couple of thousand and have Sixdog out of your hair forevermore, or pay now, and the next time, and the next time? Hell, every owlhoot in the territory will hear of this and think the railroad easy pickin's. Not to speak of the fact that Sixdog will go back to the trough regular."

Again Flannigan turned to stare out the window; then he looked back. "Bring me Chaco's head."

"Then give me the coin."

"I'll have to go into town. Come on, and we go to Stockmen's and Merchants' and I'll draw the money."

"Can't."

"Why not?"

"Not welcome in the city."

"You already have a run-in with the law?"

"Flannigan, if you want Chaco's head, you'll bring the money over to Daisy's, where I'll be packing up my bedroll and sayin' my good-byes."

"All right, all right, I'll be there within the hour."

Kane spun on his heel and headed out, then hesitated, and turned back. "Better yet, bring me this list." He fished in his shirt pocket and came up with a paper, walked back, and handed it to Flannigan, who read it.

"I ain't your damn houseboy, McCreed."

"I can't go into town."

"All right. I'll be there in a couple of hours."

"And make sure it's good sound stock, no plugs . . . and sound tack to go with them. Two fine packsaddles and panniers, lead-ropes, and hobbles. I can't be dragging some crow bait on this ride—nor can I spend time every morning trying to run them down—and bring me receipts and the balance of the money, in gold."

Flannigan shook his head. "Damn, you sure you're not kin to Old Man Hawthorn? You can be an insufferable sumbitch. You got lots of demands."

"Don't be callin' me your family names. You're the one wants Chaco's head."

Kane stood on Daisy's plank porch with Daisy at his side, studying the stock Morris Flannigan had purchased. The horse was a fine deep-chested buckskin that looked almost as good as the bay Kane had been riding since he got out of Deer Lodge. The first mule was a gray, short in the withers and loins, but deep and strong appearing. It was the second mule he questioned. "By all that's holy, that's the ugliest damn hammerheaded mule I've ever had the displeasure to feast my eyes upon. Would you call that a purplish color, or what?"

"Own," Flannigan said. "You done own him, not merely view. And I'd call that a blue roan . . . sort of."

"And you'd say pigs fly, if it was to your advantage."

Morris gave a "harrumph," but said no more.

As they talked, and glanced through the goods, Kane counted up the receipts and compared it to the coin Flannigan had handed him. "You're short five dollars," he growled.

"The hell. I told you I was taking five dollars out for the cigars you pilfered off'n my desk."

"Five cents would be more like it."

"It was your call, and I'll bet they're smoked up."

Daisy walked down off the porch and took the roan mule's cheeks in both hands, and kissed him on his soft muzzle. "Why, I believe this is a fine animal. Ugly is not always as ugly does. Take my Myron as an example. He was not blessed with a fine gentle appearance, but I've never been treated finer by a man."

"The trail will tell," Kane said. Gathering up two canvas bags full of supplies, he began distributing them in the panniers, already riding in the packsaddles. When finished, he tarped them, threw a diamond hitch over them, and cinched them down, then dug in his pocket and handed a twenty-dollar gold piece to Daisy.

She refused it.

He stepped forward, and tried to drop it down the front of her low-cut gown.

She stepped back, and shook a fist at him. "Kane McCreed, you force that on me and you'll be gettin' ten fingers across your ugly Irish mug in the way of change. I warn you, I kick harder than that old mule."

Kane laughed, then began to recount what he'd taken from Daisy's well-stocked larder. "Let me see. Two sides of bacon, a small ham, five pounds of Arbuckle's, five pounds of flour, a bag of salt, a bag of sugar, five pounds dried beans, a quarter pound of hard candy, two woolen blankets, two dozen hardtack biscuits, a small frying pan, and a bucket . . . and you won't take twenty dollars?"

"You worked four full days, mending things gone wantin' since Myron was shot down right here in this road."

"I'm a fair hand," Kane said with a crooked grin,

"but I ain't no dentist nor undertaker, so I'm not worth five dollars a day."

"You best be," Flannigan muttered. "It'll be more like five hundred a day, you win this ride."

Daisy turned serious. "You bring back that blood money you're after, and you can treat me to a week down in Denver City, with you along to tote my bags. You'll look right fine in a boiled shirt and paisley cravat."

"You've got a deal, Daisy—'cept maybe for the stiff-necked shirt." Kane swung up into the saddle, then pulled the Winchester rifle from its scabbard and examined it. "This'll do." He turned to Flannigan. "The Sharps is in the packsaddle? And the sidearm?"

"A brand-new .45-caliber Peacemaker. I had to settle for a .45-70 Springfield, Infantry length. They didn't have a .45-90 Sharps, and don't know when they will. But the Springfield should be good for five hundred yards, if your eye is that good."

"It got adjustable sights?"

"It does."

"That's second best to a Sharps, and yes, my eye is just fine with a long arm. You did well, Morris."

Flannigan added, "And there's two boxes of shells for each firearm, but I didn't know what that strange thing on your hip fires."

"This is a Bland-Pryce, made in England. It's point-five-seven-seven caliber, and will knock a buff down if you hit him in the right spot. I got a bullet mold, brass, primers, and powder, and can take care of it myself. I took it all off a Reb colonel down at Averysboro."

"Good for you, bad for him, I'm sure. Then that's three hundred rounds total, plus what you make yourself."

Kane nodded, thinking that if he needed more than

one box for each weapon, he probably wouldn't have to worry about coming back at all.

Forty yards up the road, between Daisy's and the town, was another saloon and bawdy house, far less respectable than Daisy's. Kane noticed someone familiar, sitting on one of a pair of stools made from a cut-in-half hogshead barrel. He was watching them, overly interested.

"Be safe," Daisy said, reading his mind about the danger. She then walked back up on the step so Kane couldn't see that her eyes were beginning to moisten.

Kane merely nodded, and gigged the buckskin, who set out in a brisk walk, followed by the string of three.

He got a short way, before Flannigan yelled to him. "Kane, bring me Chaco's head!"

Kane waved over his shoulder without turning, and gigged the buckskin again, until it broke into a lope.

The string followed, without trying to pull his arm out of joint.

As they passed the man on the front porch, he lowered his head, pretending to be dozing, but Kane recognized him nonetheless. It was one of Gratsworth's beer-barrel deputies.

Kane figured he might as well test the animals and attack right now. Better now than when he might have a dozen bloodthirsty half-breeds, hounds of hell, riding hell-bent-for-leather after him—or the city marshal of Cheyenne.

He avoided riding through town, rather taking a trail down the creek, then cutting north around the town before he picked up the stage road. He was only a mile out of town when he checked his back trail in the relatively open country, and saw three riders, a half mile behind.

At the first creek bottom, he cut off the trail, heavily traveled this near Cheyenne, and made his way up the creek until he came to a spot where he could hide the string; then he came back down the creek bottom to watch the crossing. As he suspected, Gratsworth and his deputies followed him, in no hurry to catch up, merely seeing who he might meet up with.

Old Gratsworth seemed a lot more interested in catching Killian than avenging his bent finger.

Kane stayed off the trail for more than a mile, then found his way back to it. He had no idea if he was in front or back of those doggin' him, and didn't much care. He had no worries about what they'd find up ahead.

He'd ridden three hours, when a horsebacker gigged his mount out from behind some brush, blocking his way.

The Bland-Pryce was smoothly in hand, leveled at the man's belly, before Kane realized it was his little brother Killian, who, in fact, although younger, was a half head taller than Kane and outweighed him forty pounds. His hair was reddish blond and his eyes were blue, where Kane was a true redhead with green eyes. Kane had an almost clear complexion, and Killian got the freckles that normally went with the true redhead. And where Kane was stoic, Kill almost always carried a smile at the ready.

"You took your jolly good time," Killian said.

"Couldn't leave before all the good whiskey was drunk, and all the ladies loved."

"And me eatin' beans and drinking pond water."

Kane chuckled. "If you weren't such an ornery cuss, half the country wouldn't be reaching for weapons at the mere mention of your name."

Kill fell in beside him on the trail. "Good-looking buckskin and gray mule, but that's a by-all-that's-holy ugly damn knock-kneed mule. Ma had a dress about that color."

"Purple?"

"That's it. Damned if he ain't a light shade of purple."

"Here," Kane said, handing his brother the lead-rope. "We'll break 'em up tomorrow and trade off leading one and then two."

"That's fine. You must'a wrangled some gold out of Flannigan."

"I didn't win this gear in a poker game. I got a five-hundred advance.

"Did you see anyone else on the trail?" Kane asked.

"I did. A butt-ugly city marshal and his two deputies came traipsing by a half hour ago. The damn fool was singing a hymn at the top of his lungs. All I could do not to make a savings deposit in their ugly hides—I got cut-up dimes in this scattergun. Nice of you to lead them my way."

"If you're so damn stupid to be catched by the likes of them, then you deserve it."

Killian laughed. "They rode by fifty feet from me in the brush, and were so busy watching track and keepin' time to the melody they didn't see me. They were lucky. . . ."

"Lucky?"

"Lucky they didn't look up. I had the drop on them." He patted the double-barrel scattergun he had stowed in one of two saddle scabbards.

"Could be they was lucky. Even you could hit them with that blunderbuss." Kane guffawed, then got serious. "We best leave the trail soon. Those lazy Biblespoutin' louts wouldn't call you on unless they had you three to one—"

"There was only two or three of them. Hardly worth messin' with," Kill said with a guffaw.

"—and they won't ride so long that they'll be late to dinner . . . they had no bedrolls. We'll come face to face with them, we stay on the trail, and they might shoot better than they fistfight or love the Lord. I hear you did some damage to one of their brethren."

"I hope so. He was right uncomplimentary and tried to back up his insults with a sap. He gave it a go with the sap, but I caught him up and twisted his arm so as it bent the wrong way." Killian gave his heels to the big grulla he rode, moving the animal and the string up into a single foot. "Let's get this done, brother. I got a lady waiting for me in Bozeman."

"Yeah, that soiled dove might fly away, you don't clip her feathers," Kane yelled after him, falling in to eat dust, "and she'll be a lot more sweet on you, should your pants be fallin' down 'cause your pockets are loaded with gold."

"How long you figure?" Kill asked, having to shout back over his shoulder.

"We're a half day's ride to the North Platte, then a day or two—hard days—to Greybull, where we might pick up Chaco's scent. And that's if the weather holds. And keep your voice down; even those city boys could hear you, bellowing like a bull calf lookin' at becoming a steer."

"Can't think of a worse way to end your youth," Kill said, but his voice was low.

As they rode on, Killian, who was renowned for his rough, untrained, but still fine tenor singing voice,

began a quickly-paced, slightly personalized ballad to
go with their gait.

> Instead of spa, we'll drink brown ale
> And pay the reckoning on the nail;
> No man for debt shall go to jail
> From Garryowen in glory.
>
> We'll beat the bailiffs out of fun,
> We'll make the mayor and sheriffs run,
> We are the boys no man dares dun
> If he regards a whole skin.
>
> Our hearts so stout have got no fame
> For soon 'tis known from whence we came,
> Where'er we go they fear the name
> Of the McCreed boys in glory.

Chapter 5

Chaco moved down from the ridge below the tall needle rocks, where he had a man posted to watch the narrow canyon, almost a cleft, leading to the cave. There were places in the lower canyon where the horses had to find a trail in the creek bottom in order to move upstream. But it widened to a hundred paces near the cave entrance.

The remaining four of his men and his prisoners lounged near a hot spring that fed the trickle that became a series of potholes full of trout, shaded by alders and river willows, before it dumped into the barranca. The slopes of the canyon were dotted with pines, and the occasional deep cut with aspens.

A couple of hundred paces above them, the canyon widened into a meadow that would serve the stock for a month, and another seep in the mountainside offered water before it disappeared again into the canyon bottom. Above the meadow, through two aspen groves, a pair of rocky game trails led up and out of the canyon, between towering needles of rock that marked the ridge.

Some of them rose two hundred feet with slick sides that were insurmountable.

Good escape routes.

It was a fine place that had been used by the Shoshone for time untold to rest and water and graze their stock. The canyon was too rough for travois travel, so only hunting camps had resided there. Villages had been resigned to the broader canyon below.

The cave itself was wide and four times a man's height in the main room, with an opening only wide enough that a horse could pass. The floor of the cave was covered with fire rings, and the walls with ancient paintings. At nightfall and daybreak, the opening became a rush of bats, but they sought the dank darkness of the deep cave, and were no bother during the daylight hours.

When Chaco neared the canyon opening, he stopped dead still and watched the woman. Teacher, seeing his hungry eyes, had convinced him to leave her be, as the white man would not hunt them with much diligence if it was only money he took. But should Chaco take what he wanted from her, then Teacher claimed they'd hunt him to the end of the earth. There was something about an Indian lying with a white woman that seemed to make the white man wild with rage.

Chaco was not sure he understood this, but the old man, Teacher, had yet to lead him astray.

He would wait, as the gold, and the guns and whiskey it would buy, were far more important than his hot loins.

One of the men with him, Black Eagle, was a cousin, a pure Shoshone who'd been banned from the tribe for killing his own brother; three of the others, Spotted-Horse Harry, Tom Badger-Hat, and Crooked-Arm Charley, were half-breed outcasts like himself; and the fourth was Teacher, a white man who'd taken Indian ways.

So far, Chaco had ruled them with an iron hand and fast knife, but they were an unpredictable bunch. Having women in the camp who could not be taken was putting a strain on everyone.

Chaco cut his eyes away from the woman and surveyed the bunch. Two of the three half-breeds, Spotted-Horse Harry and Tom Badger-Hat, were together, playing the stick game, grunting and occasionally laughing. Teacher was dozing, after taking a few hits from his jug. Crooked-Arm Charley was up on the ridge, posted as lookout, where he could lean back against the base of one of the needles and be protected from the north wind that had a tendency to howl across the continental divide in the distance. Teacher was sleeping under a ledge, his jug close at hand. Black Eagle was kneeling on his haunches, whittling, but his eyes were on the woman, the one who Chaco found himself watching much too much.

As Chaco neared, he kicked a pile of rocks, pelting the kneeling Black Eagle.

"Hey, why—"

"I read your thoughts, Black Eagle. Keep your mind on the gold, not the women. Go up, relieve Charley, and your busy eyes can watch for the bluecoats."

The Army had come very close to finding them two weeks before, but had ridden on past the narrow opening to the canyon as the outlaws had left a false trail that took the bluecoats far up the main canyon to a rock ridge, where the track disappeared.

Black Eagle was a tall man, a head taller than Chaco, but he respected Chaco's quick knife and feared his unpredictable temper. He stood slowly, scowled at Chaco, and moved away toward the trail up to the ridgetop, then paused and looked back. "Woman no damn good. Eat, sleep, mess with hair."

"White woman," Chaco answered, "probably no good in the lodge. We will raid your brother's camp and you can steal his woman, after we get the gold."

Black Eagle's eyes flared in anger. He did not like to be chided about his brother, and the woman, his brother's wife, who had caused him to be shunned by the tribe. He glared, but then turned and began the long climb up to the ridgetop.

Chaco shook his head and wondered how long it would be before one of the others threw one of the women to the ground.

The man, Potts, had been taken because he was the best-dressed of any of the passengers, as was his wife, who wore a yellow gown and carried a matching parasol. He was a small man who Chaco figured he could crush with one blow; otherwise he would have killed him while still on the train as he'd killed others. Something had made him spare this man, as he'd thought he'd have family who would fear for him, and pay handsomely even if the railroad refused the ransom demands.

And he'd been right, as the man had caused no trouble. In fact, he'd been some help, gathering wood almost every day.

There was little risk in even sending him out alone for the task, as they had his woman, a plump little lady with rosy cheeks, and a clinging three-year-old daughter. The little girl wore a matching yellow dress, trimmed in lace.

The other three hostages were all women. Mrs. Vivian Flynn, Mrs. Marybeth Pettersen, and Mrs. Angela Bolander.

The woman known as Flynn had a husband who had fought hard, but gone down under the half-breeds' hail of gunfire. She was the most beautiful of the women prisoners, with long light colored hair that reached to her waist, when she let it flow down her back, and eyes the color of a high mountain lake. She was also the most trouble and biggest threat. Chaco had noted early on that her eyes kept searching, like a nervous mink, always looking for a way to escape. He was surprised that she had yet to bolt and run, or try to sneak out of the camp at night.

He could track her down easily had she done so, but still, he was surprised she hadn't tried.

The woman known as Pettersen was also easy to look upon, young, smooth-skinned, and fair-haired, but she would do exactly as told. She kept her eyes lowered. She was dressed in a plain gray dress with high-button shoes, and he'd only taken her because of her youth and fair appearance.

The other woman, who called herself Bolander, was plump and loud, but she wore fine jewelry, and Chaco figured someone must hold her in high regard and would pay. So he'd dragged her along, kicking and screaming. Like all prisoners, she'd calmed down when she realized she must save her breath. When they had complained, Chaco had made them dismount and walk, and it hadn't taken long before they had learned not to complain.

Still and all, he would be happy to be rid of them, and hoped it would be soon, before he had to kill one of his men for dragging one of the women to the ground, or before he did so himself.

Like the others, watching the women move about the camp, and not using them, was becoming a chore for him.

Vivian Flynn had quickly discovered that it was to her advantage to keep quiet, to do exactly what the wide-faced Indian who seemed to run things said, and not to let her eyes meet those of any of her captors. When she had, they'd looked hungrily at her, finding her light hair and skin fascinating, and it had made her spine go cold.

She rose from the rock she'd been perched upon, where she'd been teaching nursery rhymes to the little Potts child, Cassandra, moved down the trickle of water away from the source to where it began to cool, and dipped a handful and drank. They had been captors of these savage men for almost a month, yet she had been unharmed, other than taking a blow to the shoulders from a stout limb when she hadn't moved fast enough to please one of them.

And that had caused a fight among them, a fight that ended with the one who called himself Chaco shoving the point of his knife under the chin of the man who'd struck her.

But she wondered, as she moved back to her rock, how long it would be before he allowed one of the others to molest her, or did so himself. He had eyes like a cougar, cold and unflinching, with a touch of fire upon occasion. She had never looked upon a man who caused a cold chill down her back when she did so, but this Chaco racked her backbone as if she were watching the rope snap taut at a public hanging.

For the thousandth time, she said a silent prayer to be delivered from this place and these terrible captors.

Please, God, let someone come and take me away from this.

One thing about the Rockies in the spring. If you don't like the weather, wait five minutes.

It had been mild when Kane had left Cheyenne, but since he'd met up with Kill, the worm had turned, and the sky was growing cloudy and unsettled as they neared the higher mountains. A little rain was not a bad thing, as it would help obliterate their trail. The further they got from Cheyenne, the wilder the country, and the odds of theirs being the only track on the trail grew higher and higher.

They'd kept careful watch and eventually, when Kane's buckskin had angled his ears forward, they'd reined well up off the trail and watched the Cheyenne city marshal and his two deputies pound on by, as Kane had anticipated, hurrying to get back to a warm fire and a Bible, the reading of which would be encouraged by a bottle of whiskey to warm the gullet and dull the mind.

Finally, Kane and Kill began to see lightning in the distance; then the skies opened, and the sprinkle became rain, and began to come in wind-whipped sheets. Both of them had slickers, and they rode on until the horses began to shy with the thunderclaps and it was all they could do to keep them strung out.

Finally, Kane gave up and turned off the trail into a narrow canyon, worked his way a half mile up through thick stands of alder, and found a ledge where both they and the stock could get out of the weather. It had been used before, as half a fire ring came out from the rock, and it was blackened above, and there were even a few sticks of wood left in a neat pile.

In moments they had the stock unsaddled and staked and a fire going. This was a storm they had to wait out.

If they could.

In the canyon bottom, not forty feet from where they huddled, was a small but growing creek. It had doubled in size from the time they'd entered the cleft, and was still swelling.

* * *

A hundred and fifty miles from where Kane and Killian camped out of the rain, Chaco Sixdog, his five men, and his six hostages cowered in the cave to get out of the sudden snowstorm. Unlike the big, dry flakes of winter, these were wet and miserable, sleetlike; they soaked you immediately, and chilled you to the bone.

Up above the camp a few paces, the hot spring roiled, belching huge billows of steam into the cold air.

The fire in the cave, normally only large enough to accommodate a small Dutch oven, was built up and roaring. None of the train passengers had been allowed to bring anything other than what they were willing to carry, and the spring gowns of the women and city suit of the man were hardly enough for weather of even the mildest sort.

The six of them were given three blankets to share. Chaco and his men had heavy coats and had pulled them from bedrolls and packsaddles when the storm began, and now, wrapped in them and each covered by a blanket, enjoying the prerogative of being nearest the fire, they stayed comfortable.

Angela Bolander huddled close to Vivian under a single threadbare blanket. They'd been told not to talk, unless they were working, but now the wind whistled and moaned outside, and they were able to cover their heads and whisper.

"How are you holding up, honey?" Angela asked.

"I'm doing fine, Mrs. Bolander."

"You call me Angie, all my friends do. I'm real sorry about your man. He seemed a fine fellow."

"Angie then. He was, as good a man as God has ever made." Her voice caught a little, but she steadied herself. "I wish we could bathe, but even if we were given the privacy, it's too bloody cold unless we could use the pool below the hot spring."

Angie grumbled, "And those heathens would come peeking if you tried."

"Do you think they've asked for a ransom?"

"I do. I overheard the boss and the old man talking before they rode out of camp the last time, and they was writing a note. You got folks who'll send money for you?"

Vivian smiled inwardly. "I have some folks back in Illinois, but who'd know to contact them, even if they had the money to send?"

"Then I guess it's the railroad they're after. At first I feared they took us as slaves and we'd end up in some Indian camp, being poked and prodded by the women with a sharp stick, or by the men with something worse . . ."

"God, that's a terrible thought."

"There's worse things, lass. Staying alive is the first thing to worry about."

"Angie . . . Angie, I thought of killing myself. When they shot Shamus down . . . I just thought I didn't have anything to live for."

Angie found her hand under the blanket, and gave it a squeeze. "Trust me, child, there will be some light in this darkness, and if it doesn't come soon, we'll force it."

"How so?" Vivian asked.

"I've got some ideas, but I'm not ready to tell them yet. You game for getting out of this mess?"

"Any way we can. Any way," Vivian said, then felt the toe of a boot bury in her side.

"Stop that damn yapping under there, or one of you will be without a blanket."

The women remained silent as Vivian fought the tears from the pain of the kick, but she didn't cry, only began to get truly angry. It was the first time since Shamus had been shot down that she let anger overcome her grief, but it did.

She hoped Angie came up with a good plan, and soon.

If she didn't, Vivian swore to herself that *she* would. In fact, the storm would cover their escape, if they could survive it. But that path might lead out of the frying pan and into the fire. Then again, what could be worse than what they were going through?

She raised her head and caught the eye of Chaco Sixdog, sitting across the fire, staring at her. The light from the flames flickered on his dark face and reflected in his deep-set ebony eyes, as if he were staring out of the rim of Hades. He was a wolf, eyeing a wounded rabbit.

That could be worse . . . far worse, she thought, and immediately lowered her eyes as a shiver coursed down her spine.

Chapter 6

Flannigan had almost made it out of his office early that evening, when his exit was blocked by a huge man filling his doorway.

The thick-necked man hunkered over Flannigan's desk had walked through the rain straight from the departing train to the station, then, finding out what he wanted to know, stomped through the mud to Flannigan's train car/office.

He'd left a trail of muddy boot tracks across the green carpet, bothering neither to apologize for the affront nor to remove his wide, flat-brimmed hat. He'd finished berating the railroad, and was now making demands.

"I vant you to hire a man to guide me. A hard man you could drive a nail into and he vouldn't so much as flinch."

Flannigan sat back in his chair and eyed the roughly dressed farmer. He was as big around as a hogshead barrel, taller than Flannigan, with tree trunk arms that filled his coat sleeves, hands like hams, and fingers the size of corncobs. He looked like he'd be hell behind a team pulling a plow, but the last thing he looked like was a horsebacker who could ride down a bunch of wild plainsmen.

"Set down and have a cigar, Mr. Pettersen," Flannigan said, trying to placate the big man.

"Got no time for sittin' and smokin'," he said, hunkering even further over the desk. "I got to get after my woman. You got a man to hire?"

"Set a spell. This railroad already has men out hunting those abducted by the heathens—capable, well-trained plainsmen and mountain men who know the country. I guess if you want to join the chase it's up to you. But you got to buy stock, packs, and grub, and the railroad won't be sponsoring those expenditures. You won't be on the trail until morning, at the earliest. Fact is, were you as smart as you look, you'd leave this up to the railroad. We got men out—"

"The railroad is the cause of this, Flannigan. If it wasn't for all those railroad pamphlets talkin' about the paradise in the West, my Marybeth would be home cookin' and ironin' and helpin' with the milkin'. Now I got to go fetch her back."

"She run off, did she?" It was all Flannigan could do not to smile, but as big as this farmer was, he didn't think it wise, and suppressed it. Instead, he furrowed his brows disapprovingly.

"Not yer business, Flannigan. You got a man, or not?"

"You might try Daisy's, over across the tracks. There's some hard men hang out there. If not, walk on into town and go to Monnihan's Livery. That old man knows everybody coming and going, and he'll put you onto something. But it's you'll be doing the hiring . . . not the road."

"I vant a map to this Greybull Stage Station. You draw it for me?"

"I will do that. Stop back in the morning and I'll have it, if you haven't come to your senses by then."

Pettersen just eyed him coldly, then turned on his heel and managed to fit his wide body through the door onto the landing.

Flannigan rose and glanced out the train window to see Pettersen leaping across the rails on his way to Daisy's. For a big man, he was light on his feet.

Wonder how the farmer will do, looking down Sixdog's gun barrel, Flannigan thought. Then he decided that was the farmer's problem. *And it sounds like he's got a wife who doesn't want to be found.* Flannigan moved back to his desk, then looked out the windows on the other side to see three reporters coming his way.

He sighed deeply, retook his seat, and lit up a fat cigar.

It was dead dark by the time they had the camp to their liking and, with the only light from the occasional lightning flash and the wee fire, Kane had a frying pan full of sliced bacon popping and spitting grease, while rain splattered the rocks between them and the rising creek.

Kane wished he'd added a couple of handfuls of beans to his canteen so they would have become soft and could be cooked by now, but he hadn't, so it was fried side-pork and hardtack for supper.

There wasn't enough graze for the stock under the ledge, so he'd hobbled the new animals and turned them out to graze, with the rain pelting on their backs. His own buckskin and Killian's grulla would stay close, so they were allowed to graze free.

"You know," Kill groused as he lay propped up on one elbow, "you coulda brought me at least one dinner of restaurant cooking even if it was cold and greasy by the time you sought me out, me out here in the woods while you was romancing the ladies and eatin' high on the hog."

"You keep bellyaching about my fine cookin' and I won't give you a chuck of the hard candy I did bring."

Kill smiled. "I'm silent as a pullet with a chicken hawk circling."

Kane eyed the creek, which was now roaring and only four feet from where they'd have to retreat from its rise. The creek was full of flotsam, sticks and leaves, and the occasional limb. The wind still howled, the rain came in sheets, and it showed no inclination of letting up.

The horses had moved up the creek where it widened somewhat and where a half-acre meadow held better graze.

Kane used the last of his piece of hardtack to sop up bacon grease out of the skillet, and stuffed his mouth full. When he had room to talk, he mumbled, "We may have to slicker up and join the horses upstream, this gets any worse."

"Hush," Killian said.

"What?"

"What's that rumbling? Sounds like a damn train a-coming."

Kane leapt to his feet and grabbed up the frying pan and his bedroll and stuffed them in a pannier. "Ain't no train track here." He began to run upstream, with his saddle, bridle, and blanket in one hand and dragging a packsaddle by the other, and Killian, his arms also loaded down and dragging the other heavy packsaddle, was at his heels.

Lightning flashed, dancing up and down the cliff side

well up the creek, and gave them enough light to see the numbing sight of a twenty-foot wall of water roaring their way, only a couple of hundred yards above them.

"Climb!" Kane shouted, and turned to the canyon wall. Luckily, he found a cleft, and began to scramble up it. Kill was not behind him.

The water hit like the train it sounded like, but he was high enough that it only tried to wrench the packsaddle out of his hands. He leaned back, his backbone against the cliff wall, and clung to the packsaddle and his riding saddle, at the same time, working his boots to gain a foothold so he could move higher.

Finally, he got a heel into a cleft in the wall, and was able to heave upward, with a Herculean effort, getting the wet saddles and bags up.

Below, in the main channel, he could see whole trees, roots exposed, that had been wrenched from the earth, floating in the mess of water. And he could hear the crash and clatter of boulders giving way to the rush of tons of water.

Hearing the horses scream and whinny as they washed past, fighting to keep their heads above water, made him think of Killian. Where the hell was his brother? How the hell were they going to run Sixdog down without horses?

Damn, damn, damn, Kane thought. *We shoulda said damn the rain and those pursuing and camped far out in the flat.*

He shaded his eyes, trying to keep the rain out of them, and gazed into the darkness. "Kill, Kill Mc-Creed!" He yelled for Killian, but got no answer.

Well, there wasn't no hunting for him yet, not until this damn onslaught of water let up.

He wasn't a praying man, and wouldn't admit it to his

brother were he to find him, but he said a quick one that Killian had found foothold to get out of that maelstrom of crushing water, tree trunks, and boulders roaring past them.

"Killian!" he yelled again into the storm, but he might as well have been whispering. There was no hearing over the roar of the water, the rumble of thunder, and the clattering of boulders and scraping, snapping, and creaking of trees and brush being washed downstream.

He hunkered down into the crevice, and waited.

Olaf Pettersen shoved open the door of Daisy's and wrinkled his nose. He was not a drinking man, and the smell of hardworking men, smoke, and spilled beer did not entice him inside, but he needed a guide, hopefully a fighting man.

The place was full of men, laughing, arguing, playing poker, faro, and spinning a wheel of chance. A few scantily clad soiled doves worked the room, hawking drinks and other services. He walked straight to a table of six men playing cards; money, chips, and cards littered the table.

"I vant to hire a man," he said without preamble.

Only one of them bothered to look up, after he tossed in his cards. He was a long-nosed man in a city suit and bowler hat.

"For what, farm boy?"

"You fill this shirt, den you call me boy. Otherwise, it's Olaf."

"Okay, Olaf. For what?"

The others stopped playing and eyed the interloper.

"For a job of work, to guide, and maybe to fight."

"Fighting men cost a handful of money, dependin' on who is lookin' back at the business end of their six-guns."

"I go after this heathen, Chaco Sixdog, who got my young wife."

The men at the table broke into a laugh, and Olaf clenched his fists at his sides and reddened, glaring from man to man. Immediately, they silenced.

The man with the long nose cleared his throat, then shook his head. "You won't be finding no one man to go after Sixdog. Hell, the whole damn Army ain't been able to run him down. Sorry to hear about yer wife."

"I can only be affordin' one man. Who would the best man be?"

They eyed each other, then glanced down the bar to where a single man stood alone, drinking. Others had seemed to have given him extra room at the bar.

"If it were me, I'd try and hire that fella at the end of the bar. He ain't the most friendly old boy, but he's got himself a reputation for shooting first, and straight, and talking later."

The man was tall and slender, wearing a dark suit with a fancy waistcoat embedded with silver threads, and a bowler hat. He wore a single revolver, buttfirst on his right hip. His face was long and whiskered with two or three days' growth, and he sported a huge handlebar mustache.

Olaf wasted no time. Leaving the others without a thank-you or good-bye, he crossed the room, kicking aside goober peanut shells as he did so.

He walked directly up to the man, standing at his side, eyeing him.

The man, even taller than Olaf, turned and looked him up and down, then spit on the floor between them. Olaf took a half step back.

"So?" the black-suited man asked.

"I'm Olaf Pettersen."

"Like I said, so?"

"So, I vant to hire a man for a job of work."

"I'm not much inclined to plow, pilgrim."

"I vant a fighting man."

The man looked at him with more interest. "You buy me a drink of fine brandy, and we'll talk it over."

"I don't drink," Olaf sputtered.

"I don't give a damn what you do. I drink, and I'm ready for another. You want to talk, you buy; otherwise go back to those no-accounts across the room."

Olaf turned to Max, the bartender, a half bar length away. "Hey, you . . . bartender or whatever they call you. Bring this man a brandy."

"Napoleon," the man instructed. Max was a beer barrel wide himself, and not used to taking orders from customers without manners, but he eyed these two and decided not to try and give them a lesson in courtesy. He pulled over a step stool, climbed up, and got a bottle from the top shelf.

He dismounted and carried the bottle and two small glasses to the end of the bar, then advised them, "This comes all the way across the ocean from Paris, France, and is one dollar the shot. You still want it?"

"Pour it," the black-suited man said with a crooked smile. "He's buying."

"I don't partake," Olaf said, "but pour him one . . . just one." He dug into his pocket for a dollar, and came up with a twenty-dollar gold piece and slapped it on the bar.

"You done earned a few minutes of conversation, friend."

"You got a name?" Olaf asked.

The man smiled a little like a viper eyeing a fat mouse, then spoke. "I have a name. I'm Doyle Venton."

He seemed a little surprised that Pettersen didn't react.

Olaf stuck out a large hand.

"I don't shake," Venton said.

"Vat. Why not you don't shake?"

"I once saw a man shot down 'cause he shook. One fella held on to his gun hand while another pulled on him. I don't shake."

Olaf studied him for a moment, then nodded his head. "It's okay. It is a fighting man I vant, not a friend."

"I'm drinking, you get to talking, and say something worth listening to. This drink didn't buy you a full night of palavering."

"Twenty dollars the day, and two hundred bonus should you stay with me until I get my woman back. This fella, Chaco Sixdog, carried her off with some others. I don't care nothin' about the others."

"So far, you're worth listening to. Keep on talking."

Chapter 7

Kane had finally fallen asleep, lying at a forty-five-degree angle in a small ravine that ran up from the canyon below, his foot jammed against a sagebrush root to keep him from slipping down to the roiling water. His face was covered with his hat and his hat and most of his body covered with a slicker. The rain pelted down on it, and a stream of water ran on either side of him, trying to push him down into the maelstrom below.

He awoke, surprised at the silence, and removed the slicker and his wide-brimmed hat from covering his face, and was even more surprised to see the light of a morning sun lining the east and the last stars twinkling overhead in a relatively clear sky. He stood carefully and stretched, almost losing his footing, but a roll down the ravine would have been of little consequence as the creek had receded to half its highest flow, and deposited trees and newly positioned boulders in its wake. He noted that he could see his breath, so it was chilly but not at all that cold.

Kane took a deep breath, and shouted, "Kill! Kill Mc-Creed!" but he got no answer. He carefully stowed the saddles, blanket, and packsaddle at the bottom of the little ravine, removed his '73 Winchester, then hiked upstream for a hundred yards. He saw no sign of Killian, and reasoned that there was no way he could have gotten further upstream than that, so he turned back down.

He alternated, hiking, then shouting and listening, and hiking again.

He was almost out of the side canyon into the main canyon, when he got an answer, or thought he did. It was more like a groan.

Moving quickly downstream, looking in every pile of brush or mound of mud, he kept yelling for Kill, until he heard his name moaned so close it startled him. As he neared the canyon-bottom mouth, there were more and more narrow-leafed cottonwoods. He'd expected to find Kill, if he found him at all, covered by a pile of brush, or in a tangle of cottonwood branches. But he snapped his gaze up.

He was right. Kill was in a tangle of cottonwood, but this was a tangle among the living branches of a standing cottonwood. Fifteen feet up in the tree, his brother hung by one leg, that knee wedged between a sharply upward-angled cottonwood branch bigger than his thigh and the trunk. Even at that height, the trunk was far bigger than a man could encircle with both arms.

"What the hell?" Kane exclaimed.

"Kane?" Killian said weakly.

"Who the hell you think?" Kane said, and began to laugh, more from relief than humor.

"Glad you ain't no hungry bear. Get me the hell down. I been hanging here all damn night like an old hog ham in the smokehouse."

"Treed like an ol' coon," Kane said, and laughed

again, but he was searching for a way to get his brother safe to ground.

"Lord, I'm dizzy," Killian moaned, so red in the face his freckles barely showed.

"You can't free yourself?" Kane asked.

"I considered sawing my leg off, but then I couldn't take your money in any footraces," Kane said, then moaned again. "You sure as hell inherited Uncle Hiram's brains," Kill managed to say. Uncle Hiram was an old man who'd lived near them in their youth, and was called Crazy Hiram by most. "Could I free myself, I'd be sitting by the fire brewin' coffee."

"Old Hiram was daft, but he was clever," Kane said. "And you better hope I am or you'll be there tomorrow for the crows to pick. You sing a little diddy, and I'll be back afore you've finished the second chorus."

"Can we worry about old times after you extract me from this gol'danged bear trap of a tree?"

"Don't go anywhere."

"Very funny. I was thinkin' about going to a hoedown, but my Virginia reel's a little rough," Kill said, but his voice was low and strained. It was obvious he was exhausted and hurting.

"I'm headed back to my saddle to fetch a reata."

"Don't let your shirttail hit your butt on the way. I'm about to pass out, again."

In minutes, Kane was back and threw the reata over a higher limb, got Kill to fit a loop around his upper body, and put his all into it to get him up to a sitting position.

"Gol'danged leg is full asleep," Kill complained, still not free, but a little more comfortable with the blood circulating more normally through the rest of his body.

"Can you work yourself loose so I can lower you down?" Kane asked.

"Where are the damn horses?" Kill asked.

"No sign. I'm gonna sit back on this rope, you try and free the knee."

"Put it to me," Kill said.

He pulled with all he had, lifting the weight off the jammed knee, but Kill couldn't free it.

"Got to use my wits," Kane said, then tied a loop in the reata, took the free end and encircled the trunk of a three-inch-diameter alder, and ran the end back through the loop. "I got a makeshift block and tackle here . . . hope I don't pull you in half," he said with a guffaw.

"If I ever do get out of here," Kill said, "I believe I'll black both yer ugly eyes."

"Then maybe I should just leave you—"

"Put it to the damn rope," Kill said.

Kane sat back putting everything he had into the effort, while Kill was lifted, wiggling and squirming, to free the knee.

"Hot damn, it's loose."

In moments, Kane had lowered him to the ground, and he lay with his back up against the cottonwood, rubbing the knee vigorously. "Damned if it don't hurt even more, now that the blood is coming back—you got a drink of water?"

"Canteen is on my saddle."

"I'll make do with this fine-tasting cotton in my mouth," Kill said with a ring of sarcasm. "You see if you can fetch the horses."

Kane walked to the creek, still running muddy, and filled his hat and brought it back to his brother, who drank deeply.

"A little chewy, but good," Kill said, wiping his mouth.

Kane coiled the reata and hung it from a shoulder,

and rested the Winchester on the other shoulder. "I'll see what I can turn up. Hope they ain't drowned."

"Glad *we* ain't," Kill said. "I believe I'll catch a little shut-eye. Didn't sleep so good hanging down-side-up."

Kill laughed, then headed for the mouth of the canyon.

Olaf Pettersen followed far behind Doyle Venton. He'd managed to buy a huge dun-colored half-draft horse that seemed to have no problem carrying him, but plodded along not even keeping up with Venton, who led a packhorse heavily laden with gear.

They had settled on twenty dollars a day plus a five-hundred-dollar bonus should they return with Pettersen's wife, and two hundred even if they didn't after thirty days or if Pettersen called off the search before. Thirty days was all Venton would commit to.

At midday Venton reined up. He had changed from his bowler hat to one with a large flat brim and a flat crown, in the Southwest vaquero tradition. And it was a good thing, as the rain had pestered them on and off; however, at this lower elevation it was a mere sprinkle.

When Olaf came to where Venton had dismounted, he complained, "We got a long ways to ride."

"Ride on, if it worries you. I'll be having my lunch in the shelter of this old shade tree."

"Humph," Olaf managed, but he dismounted, turning to care for his animal, and the big half-Clydesdale sighed as his latigo was loosened. Venton allowed the big gray he rode and the packhorse to remain cinched tight.

"Dig some of those sausages and biscuits out of that pack," Venton demanded, then sat with his back up against the thick trunk and smoothed his handlebar mustache with spit-wet fingers.

"Mr. Venton, I will pull my weight, but I don't tink I'll be doing your biddin'," Olaf said, glowering at the reclining man.

"You don't want to fetch me my lunch, Dutchman, then don't." He pulled his flat-brimmed black hat down over his eyes. "A nap will do me just as well."

"The hell," Olaf said with an unusual curse. "We got no time for noonday naps. And I am no Dutchman. I am Swedish."

Venton pushed the hat back, returning the glower. "You're a hardhead nonetheless. So, fetch me some lunch, so we can ride on."

Olaf tried to answer, but he was sputtering so badly he couldn't get it out. Finally, he spun on his heel, removed the pack cover, and fished around until he came up with a couple of sausages and some hard biscuits. He walked over and dropped a biscuit and a sausage in Venton's lap.

"Will that do, Your Honor?" Olaf asked with a derisive tone.

"A drink of whiskey wouldn't be refused," Venton said.

"The hell," Olaf sputtered again, and Venton guffawed, slapping his thighs, enjoying chiding the big man.

Finally, Venton said, "Hold yer water. You get any redder in the face, farm boy, you'll be wettin' yer pants. By the way, it's your day to lead the packhorse."

But Olaf did get redder. He stomped to a tree thirty paces away, and flopped down, leaning up against its trunk so he was facing away from Venton, and gnawed on his own sausage.

As they were mounting up again, Venton shook his head. "This is gonna be one long damned month."

Olaf didn't bother to respond, but gigging the big horse, leading the packhorse, he set out ahead of Venton on the trail, which would take them to Greybull Canyon and the stage station where Chaco Sixdog was last seen.

They had ridden several hours, Venton having long passed Pettersen and the slower half-draft horse, when Olaf noticed that atop a ridge ahead, Venton had reined up and dismounted, then disappeared over the rise on foot.

By the time Olaf caught up, Venton had a loop on a mule and was leading him back to where he'd dropped the reins of the gray.

"Got me a new mule," Venton said. "He's an ugly brute, but he'll fetch a few dollars."

"That animal has broken his hobbles," Olaf said, staring down at the mule's forefeet and the remnants of woven leather hobbles. "And he's carrying a brand, as well as a notched ear. He has a home."

"Fella shoulda watched him a mite closer," Venton said, a tight smile on his face. As he spoke, he smoothed the mustache with his fingers.

"I'll not be a party to horse thievery," Olaf said, beginning to huff and puff like a bull considering a charge.

"Nobody ask you to be no party to nothing. 'Sides, this is a mule, you damn Dutch fool," he said, then guffawed.

Olaf eyed him, calmed himself, then said in an even voice, "I told you, I'm from Mother Sweden. You call me a fool again, and it could go bad for you." He began to go red in the face again, and his voice rang with anger. "We'll lead him back and hope we come on someone."

"The hell," Venton said, resting his left hand across his belly on the butt-forward pistol on his right hip.

"You're a flat-head Dutchman if 'n I say your are, and this is my mule. I found him, I got a loop on him."

"Let's just go," Olaf said through clenched teeth, staring at the revolver on Venton's hip.

They came upon a small trickle of fresh water just as the sun touched the top of the mountains to the west, and made camp near a cluster of blooming chokecherries. Olaf staked the horses and mule with picket pins in a nearby meadow, and the two men ate beans and more of the sausages in silence.

As Venton lay back, using his saddle for a pillow, smoothing his mustache until it was to his liking, he finally spoke up. "Pettersen, I don't understand how a man could take up with a woman, wife or not, after she'd been used by filthy Indians. Only a damn Dutchman . . . Why don't you just pay up the two hundred, plus another fifty for the two days, and we'll head on back to Cheyenne?"

Olaf rolled over, giving Pettersen his back, not bothering to acknowledge the caustic remark or the question. However, his stomach roiled as if it contained a ball of vipers as he thought of what the Indians might do to his Marybeth.

Of one thing he was sure. He would not stand for his community to know that he had a wife who'd run off because of some fancy railroad brochure, and the promise of a land of gold and honey.

He would find her, if this Chaco Sixdog fella left anything to be found.

It was a long time before he fell asleep.

Chapter 8

Kane walked throughout the day, working in long sweeps across the foothills until he picked up a trail, two animals, four or five miles from where the flood had pushed them out into the wide plain, grazing away from the mouth of the larger canyon into the foothills. He'd seen a few mule deer and a herd of elk at a distance, and had had to pick up the horses' trail again after it had been obliterated by a wide track of moving buffalo. Topping a small hill, just as the sun touched the mountaintops to the west, he finally spotted the two horses and the gray mule, grazing near a small creek, now running gently. The country was generally open, with a few river willows lining the creek bottom. One lonely, out-of-place fir tree stood almost at the creek's edge, a promise of higher mountains somewhere to the west. Brush piled against its base testified that the creek had run much higher in the night. As Kane approached, the animals grazed away. It seemed the pecking order had been established and the other two were following diligently behind Kill's grulla. The big horse turned and eyed him warily, and moved away as he approached.

The buckskin's name was Charger. So Kane called out, "Charger. You and me is buddies, so you come on over here."

I guess we're not such buddies after all, he thought as the big buckskin moved away behind the grulla and the gray mule.

"Damn the flies," Kane groused aloud. He eyed the situation. He had to catch them before it got so dark he couldn't track them.

He tried one more time to cajole, talking like he would to a woman he was trying to convince of his gentle qualities. "Hey, Charger, remember all that sweet hay I piled in your stall. Remember those apples I gave you last winter?" The buckskin seemed unimpressed, again moving away with the other two.

"You knothead," Kane said, but kept his voice low. Anger was not the solution at the moment.

His concentration was totally on the job at hand. He laid the rifle aside, propping it up in the willows, uncoiled the reata and formed a loop, then moved down into the river willows, keeping himself between the creek and the grazing animals, and worked his way along until he was in front of the direction the horses were grazing in.

The first time he stepped up close enough to swing the loop, the horses trotted away, then went back to grazing. He spoke quietly as he again moved closer, the loop swinging softly over his head. Finally, the buckskin raised his head to look back at him and he let it fly, dropping it neatly over the animal's head.

He sucked it up secure, then let the buckskin drop his head and go back to grazing. The other two animals had moved away a few feet when he'd thrown the loop, but, now that the buckskin was caught, seemed unconcerned.

He'd turned to lead the buckskin back to where he'd left the rifle, when he looked at the skyline of the hill he'd come over, where he'd first seen the animals.

Four Indians casually sat their ponies four hundred yards away, watching him with more than casual interest. He surmised they'd picked up his foot trail and followed.

They wouldn't have tracked a single man on foot unless they had mischief on their mind. Leaving the loop in place, he quickly tied a Spanish hackamore with the other end of the reata and, fitting it over the horse's nose, swung up bareback. He wore the Bland-Pryce revolver, but the Indians would be little impressed with that. All of them had rifles casually across their saddles.

They began to spread out across the hilltop, then started down.

He gave heels to the buckskin, moving toward them, and toward the Winchester. He tried to remember how many cartridges he had loaded into the Winchester, six, he thought, and knew he had only five in the revolver. He never carried one under the hammer, unless he knew he was in the middle of trouble.

The Indians had closed the distance to three hundred yards—riding slowly but never letting their gaze stray from him—by the time he suddenly dropped from the saddle and gathered up the rifle.

He stepped out from behind the horse and held the rifle high so they could see it. It was a warning, but it was also a temptation, as now they had even more reason than merely the sidearm and the horses and mule to leave him staked in the meadow for the ants and the carrion-eaters.

Kane had spent two hard years guiding the Army in northern Wyoming and east through the Black Hills, and he'd taken on some of their tactics. He doubted that he could outride the Indians, who he'd guessed were Shoshone, or possibly Cheyenne, and their tough mountain ponies, particularly since he was without bridle or saddle. He reached over the horse's neck, grabbed the far rein of the makeshift hackamore, and jerked the horse's neck around until the animal fell on its side. It wasn't the first time he'd taken the buckskin down, and he went with relatively little problem.

He positioned himself behind the animal, and waited.

The hell of it was that the sun, now more than half behind the mountains, was in his face. That would soon be one of the problems he wouldn't have to face, as it would soon be tucked in for the night.

The Indians reined up at 150 yards.

He raised up, keeping a knee on the horse's neck to keep him down, and lined his sights up on one of the nearest of the heathens.

They stayed in that position for a long, tenuous minute, each of them eyeing the other, unmoving. Finally the Indian looked back over his shoulder, judging the position of the quickly dropping sun, Kane presumed.

The man yelled at his compatriots, and Kane, anticipating the charge, cocked the Winchester and loosened the tie-down on the revolver at his side . . . but to his surprise, they spun their horses and loped back up the hill.

He took a very deep breath, and, only then, felt the chill traverse his backbone.

Four Horsemen of the Apocalypse had passed him by.

He rose to his feet and allowed the buckskin to clamber up, then checked on the other animals. They still grazed quietly fifty yards away. He figured the Indians would not bother him in the darkness, when their souls would wander forever if he was lucky enough to send one of them on that long and lonely path.

No, but he had to get the hell out of there tonight. He swung up on the buckskin's back. "You're forgiven for being so damn fickle, Charger," he whispered as he moved the animal toward the grulla and mule, and began pushing them in a direction that he hoped would circle the path the Indians had taken. It wouldn't be easy pushing them in the dark, but with luck, the moon would be up soon.

It was well after midnight, a waxing half-moon a quarter of the way into its nightly trip lighting his way, when he picked his way among the debris back up the little canyon. A small fire lit his way to the spot where he'd left the saddles.

The fire was glowing embers, but Kill was nowhere to be found. The other saddle and packsaddle lay with the ones he'd placed there, muddied, but intact. He called out quietly, "Kill."

Nothing.

He called a little louder, "Killian."

"You don't have to wake the bloody dead," Kill answered from higher on the hillside. Then he added, as Kane heard him sliding down to where he stood by the fire, "You found the critters. At least some of them, I see. That other old mule drown?"

"No sign of him."

Kill limped over, almost dragging his left leg, plopped down with his leg extended, and warmed his hands by the little fire. "Damned old hammerhead was too ugly to live anyhow."

"Some might say that about you," Kane said, then laughed quietly.

"We can divvy up the goods behind our saddles and on this old gray mule. We'll make out."

"You sure you can ride?" Kane asked.

"Damn sight better than I can hobble. I don't know if I broke somethin' in this hind leg, or just tweaked it a mite. I'll make do."

After catching and staking Kill's grulla and satisfying himself the stock wouldn't wander, Kane too settled down by the fire. "My stomach is rubbin' my backbone. You eat?"

"I did. What took you so damn long?"

"They were way to hell and gone out in the foothills. I would have taken a lot longer, 'cause I woulda holed up for the night, 'cept I had some company."

"Sixdog come to call?" Kill asked, hoping they could be that lucky. Of course if it had been Sixdog and his gang of cutthroats, the odds were Kane wouldn't have come back at all.

"Nope, but almost as bad. Four Shoshone tracked me down. Luckily, I had found the animals by then, and it was near dark, and they must have had other fish to fry."

"Good thing. Get some grub, and let's get some shut-eye. I spent most of the day finding the other saddles and cleaning up our gear. Lucky I had thrown them as far as I could heave up the hillside before the water caught me, and they stayed put. Took me several hours to get the grit out of my weapons. Then I made a fire as a beacon for you, but I retreated up the hill as I didn't want it to draw in some riffraff." Then he guffawed. "Didn't work, as it attracted you."

"I'm gonna eat, then let's get some shut-eye. Can't be a whole lot of dark left."

Chapter 9

Vivian Flynn, Marybeth Pettersen, Angela Bolander, and the Potts family had been cold to the bone, but now were again in the sunshine as the sun hit the midpoint in the eastern sky.

They had survived being confined to the cave with a half-dozen savages for over forty-eight hours, and were ecstatic to be outside.

The old man who called himself Teacher had gotten rip-roaring drunk, and kept them awake by reciting poetry at the top of his lungs. He'd finished up with "Gertrude of Wyoming," which he'd explained was by an English poet.

> And scarce had Wyoming of war or crime
> Heard, but in transatlantic story rung,
> For here the exile met from every clime,
> And spoke in friendship every distant tongue:
> Men from the blood of warring Europe sprung
> Were but divided by the running brook;
> And happy where no Rhenish trumpet sung,
> On plains no sieging mine's volcano shook,

The blue-eyed German changed his sword to pruning-hook.

He acted it out in exaggerated elocution and actions, until he tripped and fell in the fire, which seemed to sober him somewhat, and he stumbled to his bedroll.

The Indians were amused—mostly by him falling in the fire.

As soon as dawn neared and Chaco saw it was not snowing, he kicked Teacher in the ribs, awakening him from a hangover stupor, and sent him hunting as they were getting short of camp meat. Black Eagle, with eyes like his namesake, was again sent to the top of the ridge as a lookout.

As soon as they walked out of the cave, Sixdog sent Alex Potts, with ax in hand, to find firewood, since they'd burned their supply almost to nothing, except for some logs too large for a cooking fire. Potts moved up the slope to one of the aspen copses. It would be no easy task, as the storm had left everything covered with four inches of powdery snow. This time, Chaco sent him with a mule and packsaddle. As he left, Sixdog yelled after him, "Remember, I have wife and whelp."

Sarah Potts and Cassandra sat near the fire, on rocks cleared of snow, and Sarah was passing the time teaching the little girl to count.

Vivian Flynn eyed them as Alex Potts leaned down and kissed his wife on the cheek, wondering why the woman looked so longingly at her husband, and held his hand for a long moment as he tried to pull away and go about the chore Sixdog had assigned him. Chaco didn't seem to notice, but Vivian knew something was different between them.

Angela Bolander and Marybeth Pettersen also

reclined near the fire, warming their hands and trying to dry out and shed themselves of the damp dankness of the cave.

Then the half-breed walked into the cave, then out and over to Vivian, who sat on a rock near the fire pit where they'd again built a roaring blaze outside the cave. She'd spread her skirt out wide to let the sun dry it as the cave continually dripped water from condensate on the ceiling, and from a few stalactites.

She was trying to brush the knots out of her long hair, and was appalled when the thick-chested Indian threw a dirt-covered haunch of venison onto her lap. "Make stew," he commanded.

"I need a knife," she said, rising, trying to brush away the dirt and blood.

Her hair, let down to brush, hung to her waist. Sixdog stepped close to her and picked a lock of the corn-silk hair up and studied it. She tried to move away, but he jerked her back with the hank of hair. He brought it up to his wide nose and smelled it for a long moment, then dropped it again, and his eyes hardened.

On his hip he wore an eighteen-inch-long knife that more resembled a machete. He slipped it from its sheath, flipped it casually, catching it by the blade, and handed it to her.

He glared at her as he did so, and she knew it was a warning not to get any ideas.

She filled a large sixteen-inch cast-iron Dutch oven half full of water, placed it strategically where the fire would heat at least half of it, and began cubing the venison. When she'd cut up half the haunch and dropped the cubes in the water, and the pot was full to the rim, she set the remainder aside and went back into the cave to fetch some salt and wild onions she had seen in a packsaddle.

She carried the knife with her, concealed in the folds of her skirt, thinking to hide it somewhere, hoping Chaco would forget he'd given it to her. She knew the likelihood of that was small, but it was worth a try.

Her eyes quickly adjusted to the darkness, and she saw that the three half-breeds, Spotted-Horse Harry, Tom Badger-Hat, and Crooked-Arm Charley, were still rolled in their blankets, but the one called Spotted-Horse was watching her closely. He was a particularly ugly man, with pox scars like those of Chaco Sixdog, but with stringy hair that stank of bear grease and knotted thick hands that carried many scars, as if he'd been badly burned at some time. But the worst of it was his left eye, now completely white with a badly healed scar that ran from his forehead, across the eye, to his upper lip.

Vivian crossed to the pack, trying to ignore the man who was watching her so intently. She heard him rising, and clasped the big knife even more tightly as she ruffled through the items in the pack with her other hand. She found the small bag of salt and bunch of wild onions—a dozen bound together with the stem of one—and, carrying both in her left hand, turned to head out.

Spotted-Horse Harry was blocking her exit. He stood with his legs slightly spread, as if anchored to the ground, his arms folded in front of his chest.

"Have you heard of Bear River?" he asked.

She cut her eyes down, refusing to look at him.

"Have you heard of Bear River?" Harry asked again with a demanding tone.

"No," she said without looking up.

"At Bear River, your Bluecoats came to my village. I only had thirteen summers. They fired on a camp of three hundred of my peaceful friends and family, with great cannons loaded with grapeshot. They killed my mother and father and little sisters, and most of my village. One of them tried to cut my head off with his saber, but only managed to give me this scar."

"I . . . I'm sorry," she said, still not looking up.

"No, you are white. Whites say much, but mean little, and their sorrow they keep for themselves, or for own kind. Put down those things, turn around, and lift your skirt."

She dropped the salt and bunch of wild onions, and this time glared at him, the knife still hanging in her right hand, hidden by the folds of her skirt.

"You get out of my way. I'll do nothing of the sort."

"Woman for breeding, and it your time."

Vivian screamed at the top of her ample lungs as Harry lunged for her.

Just as he grabbed the front of her bodice, she brought the knife up. It was so long, she didn't get a good thrust as he was too close, but the point did bury a couple of inches deep in his side. His eyes went wide and he shoved her, stumbling away. She continued to scream as he wiped his side and came up with a bloodied hand. The other two Indians sat up and eyed the scene, but didn't bother to rise.

His eyes turned to hate, and she readied herself, prepared to thrust again. He started for her.

Then he went down like a sack of flour, hitting the floor of the cave in a heap, not moving.

Chaco Sixdog stood behind him, glaring down at him, then raised his eyes to her. "You may be more problem than worth. What you do to make him crazy?"

The other two Indians lay back down, pulling their blankets over their heads, wisely staying out of the row.

"You bloody heathens," Angela Bolander shouted from the cave entrance. "You leave that lady be."

Chaco turned to her, his voice low and ominous. "You return to the others, or I will have your heart for my stew."

Angela blanched, spun on her heel, and stomped away from the opening.

Vivian stared directly into his dark eyes, her own eyes sparking with anger. "I did nothing, only came after salt and onions for the stew you commanded me to make."

"Give me knife," he said, and she dropped it on the ground, then reached down and picked up the bag of salt and the bunch of onions.

He stood with his hands on his hips. "You have drawn the blood of one of my own. Why should I not kill you . . . as is our way?"

"Because . . . because . . ." He stepped closer, his eyes cold. "Because I haven't finished the stew," she said, pushing by him and stomping on outside.

He followed. His eyes were amused when she glanced back at him, even if his lips did not show it.

"Mayhap I'll need the knife to cut up these onions," she said.

"You enjoy its use too much," he said. "Tear them up."

"Fine," she said, then she turned back to him. "That man—Spotted Dog or whatever you call him—will want to kill me."

"Do not worry. You are worth nothing dead. And it's not your death he wants. I will discourage him . . . for a while. He has been marked with a blade before. Finish the stew."

"My God," she said as she moved away again, "you are an amalgamation of the worst savages of both races."

It was a half hour before Spotted-Horse Harry

stumbled out of the cave, glaring at her, his eyes filled with hate.

Angela Bolander saw Vivian's eyes widen, and followed her gaze to the glaring Indian in the mouth of the cave.

"Sixdog!" Angela Bolander shouted from where she'd gone back to brushing Marybeth Pettersen's hair. "Do something."

"Go up, relieve Black Eagle," Chaco said with a yawn.

Harry cut his eyes to where Chaco sat on a rock. "What good having women in camp, while we sleep cold?" he asked, then spit on the ground.

"Go up, relieve Black Eagle."

"She will bandage me first," Harry said, lifting his shirt. The wound was still seeping blood, and his buckskins were stained to the knee.

"Do it," Chaco said to Vivian.

Harry sat on a rock near the fire while she fetched some rags from the pack, tore them in long strips, and tied them together. She sunk to her knees, then turned to Chaco. "He needs this sewn."

"Just bandage," Chaco said, rightfully thinking that she'd too much enjoy running a needle in and out of the tender spot on Charley's side.

She began binding the wound.

Chaco stepped up close behind her and reached down and again gathered up a lock of her golden hair, and bent and brought it to his nose, inhaling deeply.

Vivian turned and pushed him away without rising. "Leave me be," she snapped.

He laughed aloud, but turned and walked away.

Spotted-Horse Harry left camp, only to be replaced

by Teacher, returning, afoot, leading his horse with a fat antelope doe across the saddle.

Chaco walked over to help him unload, again handing Vivian the knife as he passed. "You will cut up this animal," he said.

As he helped Teacher get the little doe down, the bearded man asked, "You got the husband out fetchin' wood with the mule?"

"I do," Chaco said, dragging the antelope over to where he could hoist it up on a limb to be skinned. Black Eagle slid down the steep slope as they worked.

"He's a far piece for wood gathering," Teacher said.

"How far?" Chaco asked.

"Maybe two miles. And he's riding, not walking. I cut his trail due south of here, beyond where our lookout might spot him. He could be headin' out, wife and child be damned."

Chaco waved Black Eagle over. "Did you see the man?"

"Saw no one," he said.

Sarah Potts overheard them and rose from her spot near the fire. "There's not much wood close by." She was trying to sound casual, but her voice rang anxiously. "My husband said it was getting harder and harder to find, and with this snow and all. . . ."

"Saddle my horse, we ride him down," Chaco commanded Teacher. Then he turned and went into the cave.

Chapter 10

"Don't hurt him," Sarah begged.

"He's a cowardly man," Teacher said.

"He's not. He's going to get us help. You're a white man, why don't you get us out of this?"

"Ha," Teacher said. "I need a pull on the jug." He started away.

"You're no better than them, you filthy man, you heathen," Sarah said, her eyes beginning to tear up.

"It's the white man who has heathen ways, lass." Then he stalked away to saddle Chaco's horse, leading his own, now shed of its load.

Chaco came out of the cave wearing a canvas slicker with a bandolier across his chest, carrying a Winchester. Black Eagle had followed him in, and he too reappeared, a rifle slung from his hand and a bow and quiver over his shoulder.

"Don't hurt him," Sarah cried out, and grabbed for Chaco. He backhanded her, knocking her to her knees. But she managed to grab him by a thick thigh, wrapping herself around him, clinging. "Don't hurt him," she cried out again.

Chaco clubbed her with the edge of a thick hand until
he knocked her loose. She fell backward, hitting her
head on a rock surrounding the fire, and her hair lit up.
Both Angela and Vivian leapt for her, dragging her out
of the flames and slapping at the flames until the fire
was extinguished. The stench of burnt hair filled the air.
Sarah lay with her eyes rolled back in her head, her lids
open. Then she threw up, and would have drowned in
her own vomit had the ladies not rolled her over and
begun clearing her mouth.

"Damn you," Vivian said, glaring at Sixdog as he
stomped away toward where Teacher was finishing saddling his paint.

"What about Harry?" Vivian shouted after him as she
sunk to her knees to tend to Sarah. Her hand, covered
with blood, came away from the back of Sarah's head
where she'd struck the rock.

Sixdog hesitated, then yelled at Tom Badger-Hat, who
had finally come alive and walked to the cave entrance
to see what the commotion was all about.

"Tom, go up and relieve Harry, and tell him to follow
after us. If he bothers the women, I will slit his gullet."

Tom shrugged.

"Do it," Chaco demanded, and Tom Badger-Hat
moved away to make the long climb up to the ridge.

In seconds, the snow was kicking up behind Chaco
and Teacher's animals as they pounded out of camp, following the very clear trail left by Alex Potts.

Olaf Pettersen and Doyle Venton had kept riding
through the storm, as they had begun from a lower elevation where the rain was lighter and Olaf was on a
quest. He was worried about his hundred head of Jersey

cows, and didn't trust anyone else to care for them, even though his number-two man, foreman and only hired hand, was capable.

Pettersen and Venton had redistributed their gear on both pack animals, creating a makeshift packsaddle from a canvas pack cover. They were able to move fast, as the only animal burdened with weight was Olaf's half-Clydesdale, and it could handle even his large bulk.

In another day, they'd reach Greybull Canyon and the stage station, now that the creeks were receding and they could cross without much danger.

Venton, however, was growing more cantankerous with every mile. Olaf was beginning to believe that the gunman had thought he would give up after a day or two on the trail, but Olaf, big and seemingly clumsy as he was, had no give-up in him. Few dairymen did, or they'd never succeed in a business that called for early rising, late bedtimes, and nothing but hard, back-breaking work in between, no matter the weather.

It was Olaf's belief that dairymen were among the toughest men on earth, and he was not about to let anyone prove different. He knew he would seldom be the first in any footrace, but like the tortoise and the hare, he would plod forward, and unlike the hare, he would plow under anyone who got in his way, if necessary.

Venton reined up on a rise, looking down into a deep cut where a stream cut new banks with its high, fast water.

"Dutch," he said, his tone demeaning again, "you ready to give this up? Your woman is probably used up and cast into some garbage heap by this time."

"On to this Greybull Stage Station," Olaf said, with the same steady tone he'd taken to using with Venton.

"Hell with it. I'm heading back. You dig in that pack and pay me the hundred I got coming for four days."

Olaf's eyes narrowed. He knew one thing for sure. He'd have no chance with this man if Venton ever got a hand on the revolver he wore, butt-forward on his left side.

"We go on. You hired on for a month, you stay a month."

"No, Dutchman. I'm tired of this weather and your pigheadedness. I'm going back." Venton laid a hand across his belly and on the butt of the revolver. "You dig out my money, afore I just shoot you down like the big, dumb buffalo you are and take it all."

Olaf shrugged, swung his leg over the half-Clydesdale's big rump, and dropped heavily to the ground.

He moved back to the packhorse and dug into the pannier until he came up with a sack. He noticed Venton's eyes widen when he saw the size of the poke.

Olaf carefully counted out five twenty-dollar gold pieces, returned the poke, and moved forward. "I am sorry you decided," he said, reaching Venton's left side. He handed up the money, which Venton reached for with his left, his right still on the butt of the revolver.

Olaf dropped the coins and grasped Venton's wrist in a single motion, jerking him flying out of the saddle. He hit the ground hard and, with surprising agility, Olaf landed on his chest, pinning his arms to the ground. Venton's face reddened, both from anger and from getting his breath knocked out of him.

Olaf waited until the gunman recovered his composure, then said in that same even tone, "You hired on for a job of work, and it's a job of work you'll do." Olaf reached under a big thigh and pulled the revolver from Venton's holster. "I vill keep this till you need it. Till then, you ride ahead, and find the way to the Greybull Stage Station, so I don't have to jerk your arms off and beat you with them. Understand?"

Venton's eyes radiated hate, but he collected himself

before he answered, "I'll be riding on to Greybull. Then we'll talk about it."

"You vill be riding along till I say you go home, understand?"

"You dumb—"

Pinning Venton's arms with his huge knees, Olaf reached down and grabbed Venton by the throat, squeezing that prominent Adam's apple, smiling as he did so. "You understand?" he asked emphatically, his tone still level.

Venton couldn't speak, but he tried hard to nod his head, and finally did when Olaf eased his grip.

He coughed and coughed, and Olaf got off him and jerked him to his feet. He pushed him over to his horse, and heaved him up into the saddle as if he was light as a sack of oats, then snatched the rifle from Venton's saddle scabbard in almost the same motion. "I vill be keeping this in my packsaddle."

Venton rubbed his throat, then finally managed, "What if . . . what if . . . we come upon a wild bunch of Indians?"

"Den you better be stayin' close to old Olaf, who haf' your guns."

"Damn you," Venton managed.

"If you can't talk kind, then keep your jaw from flappin'," Olaf said. "We go now." He turned and walked back to his big horse, and mounted up. "Find a good place to cross," he said, gigging his horse until it goosed Venton's forward.

Olaf figured he'd up the pace a mite. If Venton had to worry about keeping ahead, it would be less time he would be worrying about how to get one of his guns back.

* * *

It was late in the afternoon when Kane and Killian reined up in front of the Greybull Stage Station.

The stage was in and the Abbott, Downing and Company–built Concord Stage rested in front of the station, without its team, stationary, like something dead that had been torn in half; the stationmaster and shotgun guard were in the corral, rearranging traces, changing teams. As Kane and Killian reined up in front of the hitching rail, the stationmaster looked up and gave them a wave, but returned to his work. The shotgun guard, however, stood staring. His scatter-gun leaned on a fence rail nearby, and he moved a little closer as he studied Kane and Kill.

Kane swung a leg over and began loosening the cinch on his buckskin, but Killian merely sat his animal.

"You gonna come inside?" Kane asked. "Looks like they're feeding passengers, and might spare a plate or two."

"Can't," Kill said with a growl.

"Why not? You off your feed?"

"Leg won't work."

"The hell. I thought it was getting better."

"It was, but wrappin' it around this nag don't seem to do it no good. That knee is hankerin' for some rest."

"You want help?" Kane asked.

"Nope. I'll shake it off and slide on down, like a log in a raceway."

"And fall on your face?" Kane started around the rump of his horse, but before he got there, Kill had swung his right leg over the grulla's neck, loosened the left from the stirrup, and slid to the ground. He almost went to his knees, but Kane grabbed him.

Kill shook him off. "Gol'dang it, I ain't no cripple."

"Humph," Kane managed. "You're doing a hell of an imitation. You want me to lend you a shoulder, or you want to wait here and whine while I go in and chow down?"

"I believe I'll accept the loan of a shoulder. My stomach is chafin' my backbone, an illness that a plate of homemade biscuits or a fat slice of pie might cure."

"I doubt if you can find it here. I know these folks, and this old witch will probably make us eat nothing but trotters."

"Never much liked pig's feet," Kill managed, looking a little distraught.

Kane laughed, loosened the girth on Kill's grulla, then gave his shoulder to Kill, who leaned on it and hobbled forward.

Kane had noticed the shotgun guard paying close attention to them, but the man went back to work when they limped toward the house without pulling their Winchesters from saddle scabbards.

Knocking on the door, even though he heard raucous voices inside and knew that the station was all but a public building, Kane waited until a squat robust woman answered the door. "Why, I declare, if it isn't Kane Mc-Creed," she said, moving up close to give Kane a hardy hug and kiss on the cheek.

"Martha," Kane said, reaching out and hugging her with the arm he wasn't using to support Kill.

"Bless the Lord, how long's it been?"

"Four or five years, since you and Clarence were running Dead Horse Station in the Black Hills. I heard you folks were hereabouts. Glad I caught up with you."

"Get on in here. Let me get these folks on their way, then you two belly up to the table." She glanced down at Kill's leg, curled up behind him so he didn't put any weight on it. "Game leg?"

"Martha, this here's my little brother, Kill. He said to tell you he loves trotters."

"The heck I did," Kill managed. "Pardon me, ma'am. Truth is, they're about on the bottom of my vittles list."

"Well, sorry to say, I haven't seen a grunter to butcher in a coon's age. You'll have to settle for a fat buffalo steak."

Martha headed for her kitchen.

Kill smiled widely as they entered the room. All the seats at the large table were taken. Kane eyed them carefully, but the thirteen men, the stage driver and passengers, were little interested in the strangers and all were concentrating on the hanks of buffalo and piles of beans covering their plates.

Finally, one of them cleaned his plate, drained his coffee cup, and rose from the table. "You want to set down, young fella," he said to Kill, who still leaned on Kane's shoulder.

"Obliged," Kill said, and Kane let him lean on his shoulder until he reached the chair and could get a hand on it.

"Horse step on you?" one of the passengers asked. He was dressed in city clothes, looking like a drummer.

"Storm tried to wash me over to the Missouri and down to Louisiana," Kill said with a smile, and worked his way into the chair.

"Damn near buried us more than once on this trip," the drummer said. "It was worse up Montana way, but looks like we're going out of it now. How's the road down to Rockville?"

"It should be fine."

"Can't wait to get on that train," the man said, and headed out as the others finished up and followed, rubbing full stomachs.

Almost as soon as Killian settled in, Kane exited the

kitchen with a cup of coffee in each hand. "She forgot she had some pickled pig's feet, and is breaking them out of the bottle just for you."

"Don't you ever wind down?" Kill said, eyeing his brother.

"Just trying to keep your pea brain off'n your troubles," Kane said, smiling.

The shotgun guard stuck his head in the front door and eyed Kill and Kane with studied interest, then brushed by them to the kitchen, his ugly sawed-off scattergun hanging casually in hand.

Kane could overhear his question. "Mrs. Pettibone, you gonna be all right with these fellas here?"

He could hear Martha laugh huskily. "Mr. Andrews, I'd be all right if half the Cheyenne nation was attackin', so long as Kane and Kill McCreed was here."

"McCreed . . . That's the McCreed brothers?"

"It is. Kane's a fine old friend. Once over in the Black Hills—"

"And Kill McCreed is a wanted man."

Chapter 11

There was a long silence. Then Kane could clearly hear Martha's voice rise an octave.

"And you're a shotgun guard, Mr. Andrews, who should be worrying about his coach and the safety of his passengers and the strongbox. . . . And they're guests in my house, stage station or not. You leave them be." Kane could hear her chuckle before she continued. "I don't want Clarence to have to spend the rest of the day building you a box and diggin' you a hole. He's got enough to do."

There was another long silence. Kane saw the door to the kitchen begin to slowly open, and he rested his hand on the Bland-Pryce, watching carefully.

But the guard had the muzzle of the shotgun pointing straight down at the floor, and his eyes avoided Kane's as he brushed on by, exited, and climbed up on the coach. The driver gave a yell, the four horses and two mules put their shoulders into it, and the coach, eight passengers inside and four clinging to the roof, clattered away.

Kane turned his attention back to his brother, who had been oblivious of the conversation in the kitchen. As Killian sipped his coffee, Kane's tone grew more serious. "It looks like you're gonna be laid up for a while—"

"The hell. I can ride to hell and back."

"You're gonna be laid up a while, little brother. I'm not gonna go after a cold killer and have to worry about you."

"The hell. You'd rather have me sit here and worry about you? You're not going after him alone. He's liable to have a baker's dozen of hard men with him."

"Nope, I wasn't figgering on going alone. I'm sending a letter out on the next stage north, and calling in some help."

"From the cousins?" Killian asked.

"Yep. From the kin. At least a couple of them. I'm figurin' on the McCabes, as they were closest, up on the Yellowstone, last I heard."

"And they wouldn't turn down a handful of gold, and could probably use it, the way the cattle market is going."

"You rest here until you can ride. Truth is, Martha is as fine a cook as you'll find, and Clarence is a lousy cribbage player. Even you might beat him. What better way to pass the time, eatin' and playin' cards? And healing up. You get feeling better, and you can ride on after me."

Kill sighed deeply, resigning himself to being out of it for a few days. Then he confessed, "Truth is, I'd be a bother for some time, and this leg might not get better if'n I stay in the saddle."

Kane reached over and put a hand on his brother's shoulder. "I appreciate your using that ugly head for something besides a hat rack."

"I'll wait a day or two."

"Fact is," Kane said, "Sixdog will be coming back here lookin' for his blood money from the railroad, so maybe you should just sit tight. I may not find him, and he'll be coming to you if'n I don't. I'll be back here in eight days if I don't find them. That's his deadline."

"It'll take half that for Dillon and Ethan to get the letter and get here, if all goes just right and they ride like ol' Billy-Jo-hell."

"Nobody can eat up the trail like those two. I'll scout on ahead, and you send them after." Kane slapped his brother on the shoulder and got back to his feet, carrying his coffee. "I'm gonna see if Martha can use some help. I'll write Ethan after we get a gutful."

The more time he spent in the saddle, the angrier Venton became. He couldn't believe that he'd let some square-headed Swede get the drop on him, and that he was doing his bidding. He was tired of this, and wanted to head back to Daisy's, for a bottle of whiskey to warm his gullet, and a couple of plump soiled doves to heat his loins.

He was formulating a plan to get the advantage of the big farm boy when the stage approached, its horses and mules well lathered. Venton and Pettersen reined off the road and sat quietly as the driver slowed the team to a trot. The shotgun guard appeared casual, but the muzzle of the scattergun was held in their direction, if just a little low.

The driver yelled to them as he neared. "Road passable up ahead?"

"Yep," Venton answered, nodding.

"How far the Greybull stop?" Olaf yelled to the man.

"Three miles or so, downhill all the way, just at the bottom of this here canyon," the driver answered, then whipped up the team again.

"Maybe we learn where this Sixdog took my Marybeth,"

Pettersen said as the stage disappeared and they regained the road.

But Venton didn't answer, merely clucked up his horse to a lope, dragging the knot-headed mule behind. He hadn't said a word to his trail partner since Olaf had shamed him.

Chaco Sixdog, Black Eagle, and Teacher rode hard, up through the aspens, then south across the face of the mountain, through fir and pines, until the trail of Alex Potts, who was moving at a trot where possible, turned back to the east, down the mountain.

They slipped and slid down a steep rock face, then found where his tracks turned back south on a long wide windswept ledge. Teacher spurred his horse up alongside Chaco, who was leading.

"We should head on down the mountain, and we can cut him off. Black Canyon is up ahead, and he'll have to turn east as it can't be traversed, and west is too damn steep."

Chaco said nothing, but veered his horse downhill at the first cut he came to that would get them off the ledge. He hadn't gone a mile when the mountain bottomed out in rolling hills with only the occasional stand of lodgepole pine and chokecherry.

He again reined south, and in less than a mile, cut the mule's trail, now down to a walk.

They entered a thick stand of pine, and in a quarter mile, broke out into a wide meadow, mostly devoid of snow. Chaco jerked rein, sliding to a stop from the lope he'd kept up.

"What?" Teacher asked, reining up beside him.

He merely pointed to the other end of the meadow, where four mounted Indians sat their horses, one of them holding the lead-rope of the mule, looking down at something on the ground.

"Cheyenne or Shoshone?" Teacher asked.

"Cheyenne dogs," Chaco said.

Black Eagle pulled rein on his horse, backing him back into the thick stand of lodgepole.

Chaco turned back, eyed Black Eagle, and gave him a motion with his hand. Black Eagle reined away, disappearing into the trees.

Then Chaco set out at a lope toward the Cheyenne. Teacher again reined up beside him. "You think this is a good idea? You ain't got many friends in that bunch."

"Don't need friends," Chaco said, "need mule." His eyes remained glued on the four riders. Chaco and Teacher unsheathed their rifles, laying them across the saddles in front of them.

When they got a hundred feet from the braves, Chaco reined up and sat glaring at them. On the ground, Alex Potts lay staked out, naked, breathing hard, spread-eagled.

"That is my mule," Chaco said.

"And he is your white man?" one of the braves said, and the others laughed.

"He is of no matter. But that is my mule."

"Then you should keep rope on him," the Indian said. All of them carried Winchesters with brass-tack-studded stocks. They wore tomahawks on their waists, and two of them had bows and quivers of arrows on their backs. They wore blanket coats, with nothing but loincloths, but their calves were covered with blanket or buffalo leggings over high moccasins, and in their hair they wore eagle feathers. All of them were painted for war. The man talking had blue on half his face, and white on the other.

"White man stole," Chaco said. "I take mule back to camp."

"He runs wild, under white man. You have no claim," the brave said, and shook his rifle at Chaco.

Brave Eagle had ridden through the copse of lodgepole to less than forty yards of the confrontation.

His arrow buried deeply into the chest of the brave shaking his rifle, and he rolled backward from the saddle to the ground.

The others whooped and spurred their horses, two of them at Chaco and Teacher, not away from them.

The third man spun his horse and pounded away across the meadow.

Chaco and Teacher both dropped low in the saddle, and fired as the charging Cheyenne tried to shoot from running horses.

Both of them found targets with their first shots. One of the Cheyenne fell back across his animal's rump, but stayed in the saddle as the horse pounded by; the other slipped off the saddle to the side, and managed to hang on until he passed near Chaco, who clubbed him with the butt of his rifle, dropping him to the ground. Then Chaco spun his horse and spurred the animal at the man, who was trying to get to his feet. This time the blow came from the long knife Chaco had unsheathed. He took the man across the side of the neck as the horse dodged to keep from overrunning the man, and pounded past.

The knife swept across the brave's neck to the bone, his head falling to the side, his body collapsing to the ground over a growing pool of blood. For a second he was on hands and knees, then fell to his face in a puddle of his own blood.

Teacher was tracking the escaping Indian, who'd managed to raise himself back into the saddle, with his sights. He fired at the Cheyenne, who was at a full gallop, and this time the man pitched forward, and rolled from the saddle as his horse pounded on.

Chaco leapt from the saddle, and carefully sighted on the Indian who'd ridden away from the fight at first sign of conflict, now two hundred yards away at a full gallop, approaching the end of the meadow and a thick stand of chokecherry.

Chaco took a deep breath, held it, and the .44/40 bucked in his hands. The man wavered in the saddle, seemed to right himself; then his arms went into the air and he tumbled backward over the horse's rump.

Teacher turned back to see Black Eagle, knife in hand, finishing off the Indian he'd arrowed. Then both he and Chaco took their Cheyenne's scalps.

Walking through the muddied meadow, Teacher crossed to Alex Potts, who was still alive, but barely. The Cheyenne had scalped him, and he had a wound in the stomach.

"He's a gone goose," Teacher said, then asked Chaco, "You want I should finish him?"

"To hell with him," Chaco said. "Let him bleed out. He tried to steal my mule, and led me to my enemy."

"Then let's get back to a warm fire," Teacher said, mounting up again.

"Two more Cheyenne will give up their hair, and you will round up their horses. A good day, four new horses," Chaco said, and Teacher almost thought he smiled. "The others will not try to escape, when you tell of this man's shame."

Teacher nodded, and reined away to try and catch the Cheyenne stock.

* * *

Kane was outside with Clarence, currying and rubbing down the team that had come fresh from the stage, when Olaf Pettersen and Doyle Venton, each leading a pack animal, rode up to the corral.

Without so much as a hello, Venton commanded, "You can rub my two down when you're done."

Kane walked over to the rail fence, and looked at the mule Venton led. "Well, friend, I'm no hostler, so I won't be rubbin' down your horse, nor *my* mule . . . leastways not until you get that makeshift pack off'n him."

Venton glared at him, and moved his right hand across his belly to lay it butt-forward of his revolver, then looked a little sheepish discovering that the revolver was not in his holster. He recovered his composure, then said, "I found this mule out on the prairie, and he's my mule now."

"You don't say," Kane said, and mounted the fence and dropped on the other side. "You lose that peashooter you were fumblin' for?"

"Not your business," Venton said, turning a little red, "nor is this mule."

"Fact is, the mule is my business, as it's my mule. Not hard to recognize as he's so handsome."

"You can have him for one hundred dollars in gold coin," Venton said, but knew he had no room to negotiate, as Olaf had his firearms.

"I don't buy my own stock," Kane said, beginning to lose patience.

"Reward then, for finding him."

"I don't reward horse thieves, and you're beginning to sound like one. You're a long drink of water, and you'd look real fine dancing at the end of my rope."

"It's been tried before. . . . Was he running free?" Venton challenged.

"Running loose, but he ain't free. He wasn't free when I bought him for good gold coin, and he ain't free for the taking now."

"Here, now," Olaf said, dismounting. He stuck out a ham-size hand to Kane. "I be Olaf Pettersen, from Wisconsin, here to find my wife who was stole from the train by that heathen Chaco Sixdog."

Kane shook with the big man.

"Nice to make your acquaintance, Mr. Pettersen. My name is McCreed. We have a mutual interest in Sixdog, as I'm planning to have his hide, and get all those kidnapped from the train back happy and healthy. But that don't settle the matter of my mule." He turned back to Venton, who was still glaring at him.

"He be your mule, Mr. McCreed," Olaf said over Kane's shoulder, then eyed Venton. "Hand over dat lead-rope."

Venton flipped the lead-rope to Kane, but snarled, "This ain't over. You owe me, and I don't stay owed for long. Far as you're concerned, McCreed, it's either pay up or go down."

Kane shrugged and returned Venton's glare, but walked back and loosened the makeshift rope latigo and dropped the pack to the ground. "That would be your rig, friend. And you're welcome to it."

Clarence Pettibone had watched all this transpire with interest, and he finally spoke up. "I'm Pettibone, station-master hereabouts. Go on inside if yer a mind to. Coffee is on the house . . . first cup anyways. Rib-stretchin' meal is four bits. My Martha is the best cook this side of the Mississippi . . . maybe t'other side as well."

"After you," Olaf said to Venton, and stepped back to let him pass.

Kane noted the exchange of looks between the men—

no love lost—but said nothing. He'd heard of Venton before, and in fact had walked into a Yankton, South Dakota, saloon just after Venton had shot down a man for refusing to buy him a glass of whiskey. Some said Venton had drawn first, some that he'd outdrawn the man in a fair showdown, after an exchange of heated words. No matter what, Venton was known to have killed half-a-dozen men across the West. He was a man Kane would have to watch—although it seemed that this big man, Pettersen, had gotten his goat. Still, he'd not turn his back on Venton. But like most of those who carried a gunfighter reputation, Kane figured most of it was backshootin' and bushwhackin'.

With any kind of luck, Venton would stay out of his way.

Chapter 12

It was late in the afternoon when Chaco, Teacher, and Black Eagle rode back into camp.

Sarah Potts had come to, but had said nothing, even though the other women tried to get her to speak. She'd merely sat, staring off as if willing her husband to escape safely. Now, she rose from the rock she occupied, and watched the riders anxiously and eagerly as they did not have her husband with them. She waited, Cassandra playing at her feet, Marybeth, Angie, and Vivian paying close attention as well, as the men cared for their horses, then walked over to warm their hands at the nearby fire.

Crooked-Arm Charley was atop the ridge as lookout, but Tom Badger-Hat and Spotted-Horse Harry were across the camp from where Chaco entered, playing cards with a worn deck. Harry rose and walked over to meet them.

"You have hair on your saddles," he said.

Sarah began a low keening, her hands pressed to her cheeks. Cassandra, wondering what was the matter with her mother, stood also and clung to her skirts.

"Cheyenne dogs," he said, then turned to Marybeth and added, "and the run-away man, Potts."

Sarah began to scream, muffled by her hands pressed to her mouth, and Cassandra, not knowing why, but knowing her mother was screaming as she'd never heard, followed suit.

"God, woman," Teacher said loudly, "stop that cater-wauling. The Army will hear you all the way down at Fort Bridger."

Chaco stepped forward and, using the butt of the rifle, came hard across her already bruised skull, knocking her off her feet. The little girl began to scream in earnest, and fell across her unconscious mother.

The big Indian rounded the fire to where Vivian stood, cursing him, her gray-green eyes flashing with fire, and studied her carefully. While they were gone, she'd found a piece of sharp flint, castoffs from a spot where former Indian occupants of the valley had been fashioning arrow and spear heads, and she'd had Angie saw her hair off to a two-inch length. Nearby, twenty-inch strands of golden hair lay in disarray.

He eyed her with disgust. "Now you look like ugly white man." Then he spit on the ground at her feet. "If you look like man, you work like man. Go fetch firewood."

"I should take the mule?" she asked, hoping he'd be so foolish.

"No, walk. You don't come back, my next blow will kill the woman and her child."

"You've probably already killed Sarah. I'll bring back plenty of wood, but just because we'll need to keep her warm," Vivian said, and stomped away up the canyon toward the aspen groves.

* * *

Kane had written his letter to the nearest of his kin, Dillon and Ethan McCabe, and given Clarence Pettibone the necessary dollar to buy an express company envelope and send it north.

Kane planned to set out early and head west, where he figured Chaco to be holed up. The good news was that after Chaco and the man who called himself Teacher had delivered the ransom demand and ridden out; Pettibone had waited several hours, then followed, not thinking he'd catch up with them, but that he'd at least know which way they'd traveled. And sure enough, they'd ridden east for a mile, then circled around and headed southwest, down the Greybull. So he'd offered that much to Kane.

After a fine supper of buffalo tongue, beans, wild greens, and biscuits, they sat having coffee and awaiting a promised bowl of plum pudding.

Doyle Venton had said nothing during the meal. Killian finally pressed him. "Mr. Venton, Pettersen here tells me you've hired on to help him track down Sixdog and his wife."

Venton nodded.

"You the same Venton came over from Deadwood?"

"I am." He spoke for the first time.

"You there when Hickock was shot down by Jack McCall?"

"I was."

"After McCall was illegally tried in Deadwood, I dropped into his legal trial in Yankton, then watched the hanging."

"McCall was a fool," Venton said with a smirk. "He got run down in the street by a bunch of hicks. I was at Hickock's funeral at the Mt. Moriah cemetery. Well attended, even though Hickock wasn't particularly well liked. I thought Hickock was a bigger damn fool than McCall, playing cards with his back to the door like that. You wouldn't catch me—"

Kill puffed up a little, then spoke. "Actually, Bill Hickock was a gentleman. He was born in Troy Grove, Illinois, near where our family farmed."

"I said he was a fool, and he was a fool. He didn't look like no gentleman with that hole in his head."

Kill was getting a little red in the face, but he controlled himself. "Bill Hickock was a gentleman. And Jack McCall was a coward, like most of those who have a reputation as a shootist."

Now it was Venton's turn to get red in the face. But Martha Pettibone interrupted the exchange by entering the room with her hands full of bowls of pudding.

After they'd finished, Venton turned to Olaf Pettersen, who sat next to him. "I need to have a talk with you."

"So," Olaf said, "talk."

"Outside, I need a chaw and a smoke, and we got to take a look at your horse. I think he's going lame."

"He be fine. . . . I could use a smoke myself," Olaf said, pulling a corncob pipe from his shirt pocket. "A fine meal, Mrs. Pettibone," Olaf said, rising and heading for the door. Venton rose without a word, and walked out behind him.

The night was still moonless, but the stars were bright and moonlight was pushing up in the eastern sky. Venton pulled a cigarillo from his shirt pocket, dragged a lucifer across the box, and lit up.

"Why you tink my horse goes lame?" Olaf asked.

"Maybe a stone. If we're gonna ride out early on, you need to tend to him."

Olaf started to the barn, with Venton close behind. He shoved open the door. "Too dark," Olaf said.

A split-tang wooden pitchfork rested beside the door. Venton had noticed it there earlier.

"There's a lantern over atop the grain bin," Venton said, and silently felt for and picked up the heavy fork. He followed closely behind Olaf, who found the lantern, dug a match out of his pocket, and lit the lantern. Venton waited patiently for him to set the lantern back down.

"Now, let's have a look-see," Olaf said, turning his back on Venton, who held the fork behind his back.

As he took the first step toward the big half-Clydesdale's stall, Venton swung the fork hard, bringing the handle end down across the Swede's blond pate. To his surprise, the big man merely stumbled forward. He hit him again, even harder, and Olaf went to his knees. Another blow finally flattened him.

Venton threw the fork aside, then went into the stall, where Olaf had stowed his panniers. He dug through them until he came up with his revolver, and slipped it into his holster. Then he fished around for the poke full of gold coins. Not finding them, he grabbed the panniers, dragged them out into the light, and dumped them on the barn's straw-and-dung-covered floor. He immediately picked up a twenty-inch-long box, nicely finished and lacquered. He opened it, and found a beautiful boxed double-barrel English Greener in ten gauge. But it wasn't a poke full of a couple of handfuls of twenty-dollar gold pieces. He'd guessed before that there could easily be seven hundred to a thousand dollars in the poke.

But he couldn't prove his estimate if he couldn't find the little leather bag.

"Damn flathead," he complained, still not finding the poke. He walked over and gave Olaf a hard kick to the ribs. The big man grunted with a loud "oof," but didn't come to.

Venton went back, again ruffled through the goods, and again failed to find the purse. Instead, he fitted the barrels to the stock, and loaded a pair of ten-gauge brass shells into the shotgun. He liked the feel of it, the smell of high-quality oil and wax, and the sheen of highly polished metal. Having seen many Greeners that were beautifully engraved and decorated with gold and silver, he was a little disappointed that this hardheaded Dutchman had been too money-grubbing to lay out the gold, but still, it was a beautiful weapon.

The Dutchman moaned.

Venton walked over and toed him again, and Olaf opened his eyes.

"You gonna live, Dutch?" he asked.

"I tolt you, I'm Swedish."

"You're a damn knotheaded Dutchman far as I'm concerned. Where's your poke?"

Olaf sat up, holding his head in both big hands.

"I said, Where's yer polk?"

Olaf shook his big head, trying to clear the ringing in his ears and his double vision. "I can't see too good," he said.

Venton shoved the muzzle of the shotgun up against Olaf's ear.

"Oow," Olaf said.

"You ain't gonna see nothing ever again, you don't tell me where your poke is."

"I only owe you five days," Olaf said.

"Not by my count. I count only four days, and I'll be taking the rest of it for you jerkin' me off'n my horse and puttin' your fat butt astride me. Now, where's yer poke?"

Olaf hesitated, and again the muzzle was jammed into his ear, this time cutting it and bringing blood.

"It's in the house, wrapped up in my coat."

"I didn't see you do no wrappin'," Venton said, looking a little perplexed.

"You was too busy sinking your teeth into that tongue. I had it in my belt. When I pulled off my coat, I wrapped it up and throwed it in the corner."

"Get up. Saddle my horse, then we're going to get it. Then I got a little discussion to make come to an end, with that gimped-up Irishman . . . Killian McCreed."

Olaf did as he was told.

Kane and Killian McCreed, Clarence and Martha Pettibone were seated across the table from each other, playing cribbage. Each player would play with the man or woman across the table, then with his neighbor. They played for a penny a game, which would break no one, yet would keep the game interesting.

They glanced up when Olaf Pettersen pushed through the door, but paid little attention, until he reached up with a hand and seemed to wince as he smoothed the hair on the back of his head—then stared at a hand covered with blood.

"What happened," Martha said, quickly standing.

Kane was counting out a good hand, and preparing to peg a twenty, when he glanced up, saw the blood-covered hand, and saw Venton step in behind the big Swede.

Venton held a large-gauge double-barrel in hand, its muzzle pointed at the cardplayers.

Chapter 13

"You might lower that scattergun," Kane said evenly.

"I might, but then again, I might not."

All three of the men rose to their feet, staring at the man in the doorway.

"Go over and get the poke," Venton snapped.

Olaf looked back over his shoulder. "I only owe you a hundred."

"Not by my figuring," Venton said. "Now get the poke, afore I cause Mrs. Pettibone to have to clean your guts off'n her floor."

Olaf nodded slightly, then crossed to a corner where he'd hung the coat on a rack.

"What's going on?" Kill asked, laying a hand on the butt of his revolver.

"The next man who puts a hand on his piece gets a load of buckshot in his liver."

Kill removed his hand, letting his arms hang loosely.

"You a common thief?" Kane asked.

"I ain't a common anything," Venton said, then guffawed.

No one said a word while Olaf pulled the coat off the rack, and started back across the room to Venton.

"I hate to interfere with your game," Venton said with a crooked grin, "but have the missus there go into the kitchen and fill me a flour sack with the rest of that tongue and some biscuits. I got a long ride back to Cheyenne, or wherever. . . . One thing's sure, there ain't no burg close to this place."

Olaf walked up in front of Venton, fishing into the coat pocket and holding the poke out at arm's length, and dropped it just as Venton reached for it.

Rather than stoop for it, Venton stepped back, leveling the shotgun on Olaf's big middle. "You think I'm a stupid flathead, like you, Dutchy?"

"I dropped it."

"Sure you did. Now bend on down and pick it up. Even as big a boar hog as you are, this ten-gauge will cut you in half."

As the two exchanged looks and comments, both Kill and Kane moved a step or two back away from the table. Kane said something in a low voice to Martha, and she hurried into the kitchen.

"I dropped it," Olaf said as he bent to retrieve the poke.

"Venton," Kill said, the disgust ringing in his voice, "I don't know what's going on between you two, but so far, you're making the coward Jack McCall look like Gentleman Jack."

Venton made the mistake of swinging the muzzle of the shotgun away from Olaf to level it on Killian, and with surprising deftness, Olaf came up from the floor, holding the poke by its tie lanyard, sweeping it hard across Venton's cheekbone. The gash spewed blood as Venton tried to bring the muzzle of the shotgun back to bear on the big man.

Olaf drove into him, and the tall thin man buckled as

he was slammed outside, the shotgun going off harmlessly into the air. Venton was slammed to his back in the dirt with Olaf again scrambling astride him with jaw-dropping agility.

Kane and Kill both rushed to the door, then stood admiring the way Olaf was pummeling the gunfighter with both fists. He finally let up, Venton bleeding from cuts under both eyes, his nose, and a split lip.

"Damn, Venton," Kill said, "for a man whose reputation precedes him, you don't seem so fast or deadly. Fact is, so far, you're about as deadly as a shoat still on the tit."

But Venton was knocked so senseless, Kill didn't think he heard him.

"I swear," Olaf said, Venton sputtering beneath him, beginning to come to, "you are a hard man to get to fulfill his obligation. Now, you gonna do what we agreed, or am I gonna pay you off and send you packin'?"

"Uh?" Venton muttered, shaking his head and spitting blood.

"I pay you off, you go home?" Olaf asked, deciding he was now better off without him.

"Yeah, you pay me a hundred."

"Less cost of two shotgun shells. . . ."

"Whatever," Venton managed.

Still astride Venton, Olaf turned to Kane. "You vant his job?"

"What's that?" Kane asked, but thought he knew.

"Twenty a day up to a month . . . twenty-six days now, a two-hundred bonus, we get my Marybeth back."

"He was gonna pay me five hundred," Venton said.

"I'm going after her anyway," Kane said, ignoring Venton. "All of them . . . Mr. Pettersen."

"I know dat, but now you be workin' for me too."

Kane shrugged. "I'm a-goin' nonetheless."

"I pay. And pay the five hundred if I haf' to." Olaf rose. "I go wif' you two."

"Maybe, a ways. And I'm going alone. I might have some help, but it'll be from men I know well. This isn't gonna be milkin' cows, Mr. Pettersen."

"I fought in da war, Mr. McCreed. I can handle a firearm."

"That your Greener?" Kane asked.

"It is, and a fine weapon."

"No question. You can ride along, Mr. Pettersen, but if my kin catches up, I'd suggest you fall back and let the Irish handle this one."

"When we go?"

"Well afore the sun warms the pasture, that's for sure."

Martha had returned from the kitchen and stood in the doorway, a quarter-full flour sack in her hands, her husband at her side. "Should I put this back?" she asked.

"You can," Olaf said. "Unless Mr. Venton here vants to pay you a fair price."

"You sum'bitch," Venton said, trying to sit up.

Olaf put a big booted foot on his thigh, and applied pressure.

"Damn!" Venton yelled.

"You should haf' more manners, Mr. Venton," Olaf said. "There be a lady within earshot."

"Pardon. . . ." Venton said quickly, and Olaf took off the pressure.

"That's more like it," Kane said with a laugh.

"You gonna give me my firearms?" Venton asked. "You can't expect a man—"

"You will haf' your weapons," Olaf said. "Before you ride out in the morning."

That seemed to satisfy Venton, at least for the moment.

They tied Venton's hands, tying him to a stall post and

leaving him in the barn overnight, not willing to have to worry about him causing mischief. The rest of them slept on the dining room floor, on pads or saddle blankets.

When Kane awoke in the morning, well before the others, he walked out and checked on Venton. He was sleeping soundly.

Kane returned to the house, and had the coffee perking when Martha walked into the kitchen.

"Why, I declare, Kane McCreed," she said, "if you're not as handy as a pocket in a shirt."

"You want me to check the chicken house for some cackleberries?"

"I'll whip up some biscuits while you do." She handed him a basket with a towel in its bottom. "You might check on Mr. Venton. I was worried the bears might munch on him in the night."

"Not much loss, to my way of thinkin'," Kane mumbled, but headed out to the henhouse.

On the way back, he stuck his head in the barn. "Hey, Venton."

"I'm awake."

"Hope you slept well. Mrs. Pettibone was worried about you."

"Humph," Venton managed.

"I'll get them ropes off, you promise to be a good lad and not cause any more grief. Martha is whippin' up some biscuits."

They finished breakfast quickly, and Olaf paid Venton his hundred dollars, less the cost of two shotgun shells, and then handed him his revolver and Winchester, and a loading kit.

Venton checked the loads in the revolver. "This ain't loaded," he said, glaring at Olaf.

"All of the makings is in that bag. I pulled all the bullets apart. You can reload when you're down the trail a ways."

"Venton," Kane said, this time no humor in his voice, "you keep on moving, no matter what your twisted mind thinks is owed you, understand?"

Venton stuffed the pouch in his saddlebags, and swung into the saddle; then he glared at all of them. "This ain't the last you seen of me."

Kane was real tired of Venton's bluster. "It had better be, Venton. You see me coming, I'd suggest you find a hole. I don't tire real easy, but I'm damn tired of you."

"Not the last."

"Why don't you just climb back down and I'll give you the loan of Killian's revolver, and we'll just see if you're all mouth—"

"No, you won't," said Martha, who'd stepped out the door. "You get on your way, Mr. Venton, and don't be coming by here looking for hospitality. If you're riding the stage, you just stay aboard the stage till the next stop."

Venton glared at each of them in turn, then gigged his horse into a lope.

Kane turned to Olaf, Clarence, and Killian. "I'm going to saddle up and ride out. I'll pace him a couple of miles before I head west, just to make sure he's well on his way."

"I be going with you, Mr. McCreed," Olaf said.

Kane merely shrugged. The Greener would be good to have backing him up; he didn't know about the dairyman, however.

After Kane had rolled up his goods, Killian walked him out to his horse.

"So, give me some thinking on this," Kill said.

"There was a time when Sixdog had a base camp in the Absarokas, west and a little south of here. I'd guess twenty, maybe twenty-file miles. I'll be going southwest to where the Wood River joins the Greybull, then up the Wood to the South Fork of the Wood, then over the top to drop down on him from above. They'll be watching for someone to come up from the Wood River down below, or up through Ten Sleep Canyon. He's near the Washakie Needles. In a canyon, high up, not far from the ridgetop, there's a cave. I remember him yapping about the place in prison."

"When do you expect the McCabes?"

"Well, if they're hanging anywhere near the home place and not pushing cattle up to the high meadows, and get the letter, it's a hard four-day ride, and they couldn't get it until tomorrow, at the earliest. If you're still gimpy and haven't left out to catch up, look for them in four days."

Kill gave him a grin as Kane mounted up. "Any luck, I'll be dogging your trail in the morning."

"You rest at least a couple of days. You won't be no good to nobody till yer well."

"I wish Gerrad was here to ride along with you."

"He's probably in the China Sea by now."

Olaf Pettersen came riding out of the barn, leading his packhorse. "You didn't load up your mule?"

"Nope," Kane answered.

"You don't want to take yer mule?" he yelled again at Kane.

"No, sir. I'm traveling light from here on." Kane patted the bedroll behind his saddle. "I might have to move a mite fast to be dragging that hammerhead. I got jerky, a little pemmican, and some hardtack. I can last two weeks, if I knock down a grouse or rabbit or two along the way."

Olaf shrugged as he reined up beside them. "I tink you better be takin' yer mule."

Kane eyed the big man for a moment before he spoke, slowly and carefully. "Mr. Pettersen, I ain't working for you. If I was fixin' to jerk the tits on a milk cow, I'd be listenin' close to you, but I'm not. If you want to tag along, that's your business, but don't be telling me mine, and if you can't keep up, don't be yelling for me to slow it down. You better save your breath, 'cause it's gonna be head down, tail up, burning up the trail, here on out."

Olaf merely shrugged.

Kane touched the rim of his hat at his brother, and nodded a thank-you to the Pettibones, who stood in the doorway watching. Then he gigged his buckskin and took off at a lope.

As Kane disappeared over the rise, Olaf, his arm stretched out behind him, dragging the mule, followed, bouncing in the saddle.

Clarence walked out beside where Kill watched them go. "Don't worry about your brother, he's tough as bull hide."

"I know, and bullheaded to boot. You want help getting the team ready for the stage?"

"I wouldn't turn it down."

Kill slowly limped along behind him as they headed for the barn.

Chapter 14

Vivian Flynn, Angie Bolander, and Marybeth Pettersen worked in a cold, sorrowful silence, digging a grave for Sarah Potts. She had not awakened through the night, and come morning, with the child asleep on her mother's breast, Vivian realized that she wasn't breathing. The head blows had been worse than any of them imagined.

Little Cassandra didn't understand why her mother didn't wake up, and still hugged her lifeless body as the women dug. Finally, Vivian began to ease the work by singing "Nearer My God to Thee."

And if on joyful wing,
Cleaving the sky,
Sun, moon, and stars forgot,
Upward I fly;
Still all my song shall be—
Nearer, my God, to Thee,
Nearer, my God, to Thee,
Nearer to Thee!

Teacher walked down and, as if he had not been an accomplice in her death, joined in the singing . . . but not the work.

The Indians seemed intrigued by this, and they too walked over to watch the white women bury one of their own.

After they'd sung two verses, Sixdog snapped at them, "It would be better you build a pyre and burn her, so her spirit can rise into the clouds."

Vivian ignored his suggestion, and glared at him before she spoke. "We need something to wrap her in."

Chaco shrugged. "Use one of your sleeping blankets."

"Then one of us will sleep cold."

Chaco laughed. "Yes, one of you will sleep cold."

Vivian turned back and angrily continued to dig.

Angie stopped to take a breath, and offered, "I have two sets of petticoats, and can get by with one. We can at least cover her face with a petticoat."

"You're very kind, Angie," Vivian said, and kept digging.

When through, the women, with Cassandra screaming at the top of her lungs, gently lowered Sarah into the two-foot-deep hole, covered her face and upper body with the petticoat, then gathered together and offered the Lord's Prayer.

When they finished, Vivian whispered to Angie, "Take Cassandra inside while we cover her up. It's not for a child to see."

"You've done enough," Angie said. "You take her in. She's taken with you, and you would do better."

Vivian nodded sadly, walked over, picked Cassandra up in her arms, and whispered, "Come, my sweet Cassie." With the little girl whimpering, and Vivian humming a hymn, she carried her inside the cave.

When they finally returned, there was a small mound

where the hole had been, and they all joined in gathering rocks to pave the grave.

When they were finished, Vivian again picked Cassandra up in her arms, then sat on a rock near the grave, and began to sing an old Irish song, soft and sweet, substituting the young girl's nickname for the name Colleen, to soothe her:

> From Bantry Bay up to Derry Quay
> And from Galway to Dublin town
> No maid I've seen like the sweet Cassie
> That I met in the County Down.

> *At the crossroads fair I'll be surely there*
> *And I'll dress in my Sunday clothes*
> *And I'll try sheep's eyes, and deluding lies*
> *On the heart of the nut-brown rose.*
> *No pipe I'll smoke, no horse I'll yoke*
> *Though with rust my plow turns brown*
> *Till a smiling bride by my own fireside*
> *Sits the star of the County Down.*

> From Bantry Bay up to Derry Quay
> And from Galway to Dublin town
> No maid I've seen like the sweet Cassie
> That I met in the County Down.

The Indians watched it all with interest. When Vivian sat with the little girl, repeating the song for the third time, they began to find other things to pass the time.

When she'd finished, Cassandra was asleep, but Vivian continued to hold her, rock her gently, and hum the melody.

Chaco walked past Teacher on his way to the horses, and asked, with some impatience, "How many days?"

"A week more, Chaco. It's only been eight days, we can ride out in five."

"A week, then if the money is not there, we kill the whelp and tack her to the barn door. That will make them gather our gold."

"Or half the U.S. Army, and five times one thousand soldiers will come for us. Kill the fat woman, Bolander, first."

"No, the child."

Teacher shrugged, and mumbled, "It's yer hide," then went looking for his jug.

Kane was rolled in a blanket, having eaten a few pieces of jerky and a couple of biscuits, and almost asleep. With the sun full down, he was surprised when he heard the clomp of a pair of horses.

"Hallo the camp," Olaf called out.

Kane raised his head and eyed the big man, who almost fell off his horse.

"I wondered if you'd find me in the dark," Kane said with a yawn.

"You make a cold camp?"

"I do. No fire. I don't want to send an engraved invite to Chaco and his boys."

"All I got is bacon," Olaf complained.

"All you got is bacon," Kane said.

"Dat's what I say. All I got is bacon. Bacon not so good, raw."

"Dig in my satchel and fish out some jerky and a biscuit."

"I like bacon," Olaf lamented.

"Then eat it raw. No fire."

"No fire," Olaf repeated. He was so tired, he didn't seem to much mind. Rather than eating, he rolled in his blanket, and in moments was snoring with a roar like the great falls up on the Missouri.

Kane finally rose, rolled his blanket, picked up his rifle, and made his way through the underbrush. "Talk about baiting the bears," he groused, and he rolled up far enough away that Olaf's snoring was only a low roar.

As the morning sun warmed the camp, Angie, Marybeth, and Vivian traded off keeping Cassie busy, trying to keep her mind off the stone covered mound that was far too near for comfort. While Angie was taking a turn at playing with her, Marybeth sidled up next to Vivian.

"Do you think we'll ever get out of this?" Her eyes were pleading.

Vivian had long ago made up her mind that Marybeth, blond and seemingly frail, was the weakest of the lot, if you didn't consider Cassie.

"We will, Marybeth. If what I've overheard is true, the railroad will pay a ransom, and we'll be free."

Tears pooled in Marybeth's eyes, and then rolled down her cheeks. "I only wanted to go to California, and get away from Olaf and my stepchildren. Monsters they were, and Olaf would only laugh when they'd do something mean. I have to get to California, and start a new life."

"I was on my way to California too . . . but now, I don't know."

"Your husband had a job there?"

"He had a brother there. A brother who I imagine was waiting for the train at Sacramento, and had to find out that I was missing and his older brother was dead."

"How terrible."

"They hadn't seen each other in almost twenty years."

Marybeth screamed at the top of her lungs, looking over Vivian's shoulder and making her leap to her feet and spin around.

Black Eagle stood, laughing, shaking a coup stick at her, the stick lined with four scalps, one of them fresh.

The other Indians—other than Badger-Hat, who was atop the hill on lookout—sat across the camp with Teacher, laughing loudly.

Chaco walked from the cave, and snapped at Black Eagle, "Leave them be." Then he walked over and stood glaring at Vivian. "Why you wish to look like an ugly man?"

"If you fancy my hair, you can still gather some of it up. It's over there on the ground. . . . When are you going to take us back to the railroad?"

"Never," he said simply.

"Then when are you going to let us go?"

"You have only as many days as I have fingers on this hand," he said, holding up a calloused paw.

"Then you let us go?"

"Maybe. If they have gold to trade. Maybe I kill you first, then take you to stage stop. I do not like woman with no hair. You look like dog."

Vivian turned and sat back down, ignoring him. She was sure that after so many days in the wild, she did look like an old sheep dog. He strode away, yelling at the other men, "One of you go get camp meat."

Teacher rose and stretched. "I'll go. I'm bored as a hound dog tied to a post."

Kane had ridden hard all morning, and well into the afternoon, even munching his jerky while in the saddle, pausing only to water the buckskin and let him blow. He'd left Olaf in the dust after the first two miles. He hadn't mentioned to Killian how close he thought Chaco's camp might be, afraid that he'd want to ride along.

He'd climbed up out of the high prairie, and only an occasional copse of lodgepole, into ponderosa, aspen, and alder. The mountains were high and hard-shouldered.

He'd left the main Wood River at mid-morning and continued up the South Fork, until now he could see what he thought was the crest of the mountain three or four miles ahead.

He knew the Washakie Needles were somewhere south of him, probably no more than three or four miles, but it would be a tough couple before he crested the ridge to his south and could look down upon the high narrow rocks that were the needles—and somewhere among them was a cave, a cave that Chaco Sixdog, on long nights in Deer Lodge Prison, had described as his ultimate hideout.

Kane spooked a small herd of elk, and the thought of elk steaks made his mouth water, particularly as a young spike bull stopped broadside at one hundred yards and watched him, probably never having seen a horse, particularly one with a growth on its back that was a man. Kane laughed at the thought, but not at the thought of Chaco and his bunch hearing a shot and coming to investigate.

Finally, he left the tree line behind, and thin soil and sparse grass turned to shale. He dismounted, deciding to spare the buckskin, already winded, and lead him up the last quarter mile.

Stopping to rest halfway up the escarpment, the buckskin now lathered and, breathing heavily, he sat on a rock outcropping and surveyed the country below. It was a beautiful spot, some of the best of the high lonely, and he knew he was near the continental divide. It would be far more beautiful if he wasn't quite so sure he was riding into a nest of high-country vipers.

Watching below for a half hour, to rest himself and the horse, he looked for Olaf and his big dun, and the mule, if he hadn't yet abandoned the mule. He saw no sign of him, and finally decided to make a run at the ridge.

The last eighth of a mile took almost an hour, as he kept running into high ledges that he couldn't broach with the horse. He finally found a cut, and they crossed a level ledge, where a family of marmots watched him with curious abandon, and in moments he was looking at the needles, less than two miles distant.

Checking the sun, he decided that he could make the next ridge before he had to worry about darkness. This high, the chance of finding water was nil, but the crest of the mountain to the west was still snow-covered, so with luck, the cut between the ridge he sat upon and the next would carry a trickle of snow runoff.

The two ridges ahead held little growth, only a few stubby white-cone pines on the north-facing slopes, and nothing on the slope below him nor, odds were, on the slope on the other side of the next ridge. Beyond that were the needles. He should have a clear view for over a mile from the top of the next ridge.

The sun had sunk below the continental divide to the west by the time he'd stopped to water the buckskin, then had reached the top of the next ridge. He wasn't sure, but he thought he caught a wisp of smoke in the distance, no more than three-quarters of a mile away.

Chapter 15

If the wind came up, the top of the ridge would be a cold and lonely place; not a place to leave the buckskin, as it lacked graze. He went ahead and let the sure-footed animal pick his way down the slope until they found the bottom, and another trickle of cold runoff. In a small flat, he found some graze, and staked the buckskin out so he could both water and feed.

Kane was going to reconnoiter the country ahead on foot. It wouldn't do to have the ring of horseshoes announcing his coming, if there was actually an encampment in the distance.

He checked the loads in the Winchester and his Bland-Pryce revolver, and set out at a brisk walk. Above him, the rock needles were outlined by the final glow of nightfall, and looked ominous as they rose high and blacked out the stars just beginning to flicker around their outlines.

He knew the moon would be rising within a couple of hours, and wanted to get this work done before he could be easily highlighted crossing the low ridge between where he'd left the horse and where he thought he'd seen the tendril of smoke.

After a half mile, he saw a ghost of a shadow move across a rock wall, no more than two hundred yards in front of him, and realized the wall was lit by a flickering fire that he could not see.

He toe-heeled it for another hundred yards, moving as if he were hunting wary game. Five steps, then a long wait, then five more, feeling each twig underfoot before he put his weight down. The crack of a broken branch underfoot or the displacing of a pebble wouldn't do. Not when he might be this close to his target.

He knew what his biggest quandary would be, other than being discovered and shot dead, or worse: the decision—take down Chaco Sixdog, or escape with Vivian and as many of the others as he could and save the ten-thousand-dollar Chaco for later.

No matter what he'd told Flannigan, Vivian was his first order of business. It was damned unlikely he could do both . . . not alone. In fact, it was damned unlikely he could do either, with a camp full of savages less than a hundred yards from where he crept.

Deciding to let things fall as they might, he continued to stalk slowly toward the light, until he could make out a flickering campfire and half-a-dozen or more human forms enjoying its heat.

There was obviously a hot spring up above the camp his way, a dozen or more paces, as the steam bellowed up to disappear into the darkness. Chaco had talked of a hot spring, in which the Indians had soaked their weary bones when using the camp and cave after a hard hunt.

This had to be the spot, and the women he could barely make out, in city clothes, had to be Chaco's prisoners, with Vivian among them.

Three women and a child were huddled off to one side, and four men sat around a flat rock, playing cards by candlelight. He did not see the white man, Teacher, as described to him by the Pettibones, but he thought Chaco was one of the grunting, grousing, and shouting cardplayers.

He knew another man would be posted somewhere as a lookout.

In the distance beyond them, he could see the mouth of a cave, and inside it another fire burned somewhere. Maybe more of them were inside—no telling how many.

He moved through the brush until he was within twenty-five yards of the group of women. He made out two of them, a frail-looking light-haired girl with fine features, whom he decided couldn't be Vivian, and a buxom, dark-haired, plump woman of middle age; both of them faced the fire. The other woman faced his way, and all he could make out was her short-cropped hair. Vivian had always had long, beautiful blond locks. Could it be that Vivian was not with them? Chaco had taken four women from the train. Or could it be that she was in the cave?

He hoped against hope that she hadn't been killed by this bunch of heathens.

If she had, he wouldn't rest until each of them roasted over a slow fire.

Then the woman turned, and he recognized Vivian's beautiful profile even without hair. He let his spirit soar for a moment, then collected himself. He began to inch forward, then heard footsteps behind him.

He turned only far enough so he could see to the rear, then froze in place, not breathing. Footfalls crunched nearer.

A big Indian passed within four paces of him, so

close that Kane got a whiff of his musky odor, and entered the camp.

"Too dark to see," the man shouted to the cardplayers, then walked straight into the cave.

He must have been the lookout.

Finally, Kane let the deep breath out, but even did that slowly and silently.

Vivian turned back and began playing a game with the child, where they patted the flat of their hands together in time with the rhyme they sung.

When the cardplayers lowered their voices, he made out a verse:

> The needle's eye that doth supply
> The thread that runs so true;
> I stump my toe, and down I go,
> All for wanting you.

Inching forward, he positioned himself almost in the midst of a thick river willow, and rose until he could see Vivian clearly. The other two women and the child had their backs to him.

He watched the men, twenty paces in the distance, then carefully, silently, parted the willow branches where Vivian could clearly see his face, if she'd only look up.

His eyes continued to cut from her face to the men in the background, intent on their game.

She finally glanced up. Then she flinched backward, her eyes widened, and her jaw dropped.

Kane merely nodded, then let the willow branches close and lowered himself again. He began to carefully move back away from any chance of firelight.

In a few moments, Vivian stood and yawned, then

called to the cardplayers, "I have to attend to the necessary."

One of them turned to face her, and Kane could clearly make out the face of Chaco Sixdog. He rose and eyed her. "You will not go beyond the hot spring."

"No."

"Remember, I have others, and child will be killed first."

"Where would I run?" Vivian said.

In moments, she was beside him in the river willows. She gave him a big hug, and whispered in his ear, "Thank you for coming, Mac." He only allowed himself the pleasure of the hug for a moment, then turned to lead her away.

She jerked back.

He moved close, to see what was wrong.

"I can't leave the others," she whispered.

"Viv, this is your chance to be out of this. I'll come back for Sixdog, and his crew; then they'll all be free."

"Not all of them; the Potts couple is already dead. Chaco killed both Mr. and Mrs. Potts. I can't risk little Cassie. He said he'd kill her too if any of us tried to run." She stared at him, utter defeat in her eyes. "You have no idea how much I want. . . ." She reached over and laid a hand on his shoulder, her eyes hypnotizing him. "But I can't. I just can't."

Kane took a deep breath. From Vivian's tone, he knew trying to lead her away was futile. For an instant, he thought of knocking her unconscious, but let the thought fade. He pulled her close and whispered in her ear.

"Do you think you can get them all out of camp at the same time?"

"No. Chaco or one of the others watches us every moment."

Kane started to speak, then was shocked by the sound of a rifle shot. He dropped to the ground, pulling Vivian down with him. Then another, and another, but they were distant, way up behind them, on top of the ridge or probably over it, maybe a mile or more.

"Get away," Vivian said. "They'll come."

Kane slunk back in the willows as Chaco and one of the other Indians ran to where Vivian stood, brushing off her skirts as if nothing was awry.

"Get back in camp, in the cave," Chaco commanded.

She moved quickly away. The Indian with Chaco let his eyes wander over the willow thicket, but Kane was frozen in place, and with no moonlight and little starlight, he was not discovered. He had a terrible itch to pull his revolver and end it right then and there, but killing Chaco would not end it, only put them all in great jeopardy from the others. He let the itch fade away, as he kept his eyes half-closed so they wouldn't catch the light.

Both of the men stalked back into camp.

Kane repositioned himself where he could see the camp clearly, and watched as two men walked out of the cave. One of them, he decided, was the white man described to him by Pettibone, and the other was the man who'd come down from being on lookout.

They palavered for a few minutes, kicked out the fire, and herded the women and child into the cave. Then two of them walked out of camp in different directions, apparently going out as sentries. Luckily, neither of them came Kane's way.

He backed away slowly, until he could turn and move quickly away from the camp.

In fifteen minutes he was across the ridge, and in another ten he'd found the buckskin.

He had to find out who the hell was doing the shooting in the black of night, and why.

He knew one thing for sure. Whoever it was had made damn sure that Sixdog's camp would be doubly wary.

Olaf had camped in the same hollow where Kane had left the buckskin, only a half mile below. He was cold to the bone, and built a large fire before he did anything else. He warmed his hands, and his generous backside, and only then saw to his horse. Had it been a milk cow, the animal would have received quick attention.

Luckily, the big half-Clydesdale whinnied loudly when Olaf had dropped the saddle away, and the big man was surprised when a whinny was returned from a long distance.

It was pure divine intervention, because Olaf became very alert, hoping he had not attracted attention from the camp of Sixdog and his savages, but rather from Kane's buckskin.

He slipped his Greener from where he'd had it tied behind the saddle since letting the mule go free, and loaded it carefully.

Grabbing a stick, he knocked the fire down, wondering how wise he'd been to even start it, even if all he had in the way of substantial eating was the slab of bacon. He would burn it very low until he had a bed of coals, he decided—when a searing pain shot through his side, and a gunshot rang in his ears. With surprising quickness, he dove into the dark underbrush, taking his shotgun with him, then crawled deeper, well out of sight of the fire, and stayed as flat as a big man could as two other rifle shots kicked up dirt near him. The big horse

sat back and pulled free of the brush where Olaf had
tied him, trotting away into the darkness.

Then there was nothing but silence.

Olaf moved even deeper. He pulled his linsey-
woolsey shirt off, took his folding knife out, and cut the
tail off to stuff in the hole in his side. Then he felt his
back, and found the wound was through and through.
He cut another piece, and stuffed it as well as he could
to quell the bleeding. He lay there in silence, figuring
he'd pass out soon from the blood he'd lost and that still
seeped, even with the wound stuffed with wool.

It was a long time—the moon had risen—when he
heard the clomp of a horse's hooves.

He grasped the Greener tightly, and strained his eyes.

Finally, a man leading a horse approached, moving
cautiously and quietly. He entered the camp, holding a
Winchester, cocked and ready and pointed toward the
brush.

Olaf pulled the Greener tight to his shoulder, and waited
for the man to move to where he could be clearly seen.

Chapter 16

He worried that the man might be Kane McCreed, but why would McCreed shoot at him . . . unless he wanted his poke? He eyed the man carefully . . . he was a tall man, a head taller than McCreed, but not as thick through the shoulders.

He didn't think McCreed was the kind to bushwhack, even if he did want his poke.

The man who'd crept into Olaf's rough camp found a splatter of blood, and anger coursed through the big dairyman's veins when he heard the man guffaw, and thought he recognized the voice.

Then the man laid his rifle aside, found Olaf's bedroll, stripped the ties away, and unrolled it, letting Olaf's belongings scatter near the fire.

Olaf figured he was less than thirty paces away in the brush, and there was scattered brush between him and the man's back.

Still, he raised the scattergun, carefully sighted down the Greener's double barrels with his eyesight wavering, and pulled both triggers.

The Greener bucked violently; the man slammed to his face, unmoving.

Olaf managed to reload the Greener, then lay still for a long while. He was dizzy, his head swimming, and unless he heard stirring, he wasn't about to try and sit up.

Finally, just as the moon appeared, things went black and he faded away.

Kane had arrived at the horse about the time he heard the flat crack of the shotgun, definitely a different weapon than the shots he'd heard earlier.

The moon was rising, but there was not enough light that he thought he could be seen from the ridge behind, just in case someone from Chaco's camp might be heading over the rocks to find out what the shooting was about.

With three rifle shots and a shotgun fired, they should have a good bead on direction.

He quickly saddled the buckskin, mounted, and moved away toward the sound of the shotgun blast. If those from Chaco's camp were coming, he wouldn't have much time; then again, it wouldn't do to ride into a gunfight perched up horseback, fat, dumb, and happy.

Leaping from the horse's back after he'd covered a quarter mile, he moved forward on foot, leading the buckskin, carrying the Winchester. He left the long-shooting but single-shot .45/70 in its saddle scabbard, and would depend upon the Bland-Pryce and the Winchester.

He pulled up short when he thought he saw the glow of a low campfire in the distance, but the willows and chokecherries occluded a clear view. He tied the buckskin loosely, not wanting the big animal to be unable to pull free, just in case he didn't return, and moved off into the brush to circle the camp.

Working his way up the hillside so he could look

down on the camp, he hunkered down only forty yards above the site, waited, and watched. He would have stayed silent for longer, but he pictured half-a-dozen hard men from Chaco's camp coming over the hill, and if so, he wanted to see what was afoot in the camp, and get the hell out of there.

Finally, he began his descent, moving from clump of brush to clump of brush, until he was ten paces from the fire and could make out a man, facedown.

Kane dropped to one knee when a groan echoed through the silent night; then after seeing no movement, he rose and went into the camp, hunkered low. He poked the man, whom he could now see had a back covered with blood, but the man didn't move. With a booted toe, Kane rolled the man over, and was surprised to see Doyle Venton's pale whiskered face.

"You'da been a mite smarter to keep on going to Cheyenne," Kane muttered, but got no reply, although the man was still breathing.

Then he heard another sound, deeper in the brush. . . . raspy breathing.

Kane moved again into the brush, and circled until he could see the second man, a big man, only this one lay on his back. Silently, Kane cocked the Winchester, kept it trained on the man, and moved forward, toeing his way.

He reached down, picked up a rock the size of his thumb, and flipped it, hitting the man in the chest; then he realized it was Olaf Pettersen. Kane moved the last eight paces and reached down and pulled the Greener out of Olaf's grasp, and the big man opened his eyes.

"Damn, it was you," he muttered, then closed his eyes again. Kane knelt by the big man and pulled up his coat and shirt, already untucked. He realized some of the shirttail had been cut away. He studied the wound, and rolled the big man over to check the exit wound. Wondering if the wound had blown a hole in an intestine, but not sure, he went ahead and swabbed it with his own neckerchief, then left the man and hurried back to where he had tied the buckskin.

Returning, he cut a long piece from his blanket, and bound the wound as best he could, then poured some water in the big man's face.

Olaf sputtered, and again opened his eyes, but they were dull and distant.

"Olaf, you've got to get up and on this horse, so we can get some distance between us and this camp."

"You shot me," the man muttered.

"The hell I did. I imagine Doyle Venton shot you. He's laying out there by the fire, looking like he was fodder for a buffalo stampede."

"Venton," he muttered, then again closed his eyes.

"I've got to get you up and on the horse, Olaf."

"Don't know. . . ."

Kane fought the big man's weight, but finally got him to his feet, then supported him with one of Olaf's arms on his own broad shoulders. For once, the fact that Kane was shorter than a man worked to his advantage as they moved up beside the buckskin. With Olaf staggering beside him, he led the horse to a low ledge, dropped his reins, and then had to lay Olaf across the knee-high ledge, climb up, and get the big man back to his feet. He said a silent prayer that the buckskin wouldn't shy, but the big faithful horse stayed put, and lowered its head to graze while Kane fought to flop Olaf across the saddle, then to keep him from falling off on his head on the other side. He had him across the saddle, moaning as if a March wind were howling through the white pines. Kane readjusted him so he was more face-forward, then shoved his leg over the horse's rump, and got him in the saddle, even if he lay forward across the buckskin's withers. Kane slipped his folding knife out and cut away a pair of the saddle's tie-downs, and tied each of Olaf's legs to the latigo.

"You've got to stay in the saddle, Olaf," Kane commanded, but the big man was merely moaning.

Without looking back, but expecting to hear the big man crash to the ground with every step, Kane set out, leading the buckskin, up and away from the camp.

He felt a twinge of remorse at leaving Venton still alive to be fed on by the critters. But Venton, Kane figured, had brought whatever came upon himself.

Olaf, on the other hand, even though a bit of the fool, was on an unselfish mission. He could be home by a warm fire, wondering where his wife was, or relishing the fact she was gone, as would many husbands who Kane had had an acquaintance with, but he wasn't; Olaf was here, dripping his lifeblood, trying to free her from something that neither of them had done.

No, Venton would have to fare for himself.

They walked for two hours, Olaf clinging and moaning, Kane moving up until he reached the ridge away from Chaco's camp, then down the long ridge, until he came to a thick stand of lodgepole pine, flanking a trickle of water. Half-expecting Olaf to be dead in the saddle, he loosened the leg ties and lowered the big man to the ground.

But his moans and groans assured Kane he was still full of spirit, and had yet to give it up.

It would be a cold camp, at least until morning. Kane had allowed himself one small frying pan, two palms in diameter, and he could make coffee in the morning, or maybe a jerky soup. . . . if Olaf were still alive to eat it.

If not, Kane had made up his mind that he'd go back and drag Vivian out of that camp before something horrible befell her, but if he awoke and Olaf was still moaning, he'd make a travois, and drag him back toward Greybull . . . until the big man died, or until he got him to where Mrs. Pettibone could care for him.

Killian McCreed had been pacing like a caged cat for the last two days, even if the pacing involved half-dragging a leg.

Clarence Pettibone gazed up from reading a fresh copy of *Leslie's Weekly,* only three weeks old, and eyed the young man as he walked to the window for the fifth time since supper.

"Dang, if yer not like a man about to hang come first light." He glanced toward the kitchen, to make sure his wife was not in earshot, and lowered his voice. "I got a jug of corn out in the barn. You want a shot of 'calm down'?"

"Stage is due in come tomorrow?" Kill asked.

"It is, usually some before noon."

"Southbound, it'll be?"

"Yep."

"Damned if this leg don't heal, so I can ride out . . ."

"Damned? Damn fool is what you are, keeping weight on it. You sit over there in Martha's rocker and I'll take our coffee cups out and get us a taste, but Lord, Lord, don't let the missus know."

Kill smiled, eyed the rocker, and limped over and flopped down. "Could I have the loan of the *Leslie's* while you're out?"

* * *

The weather had warmed and the snow was about gone except for the very tops of the ridges.

The women sat around the outside fire, Cassie asleep in Vivian's lap.

The Indians, except for Black Eagle, were inside the cave, laughing and playing cards by firelight. Black Eagle was messing with the horses, far enough away that he was well out of earshot.

Angie Bolander leaned closer to Vivian, and said in a loud whisper, "I'm so tired. Sick and tired. I don't know how much more of this endless waiting I can take."

"I wish there was something to do about it," Vivian answered.

Marybeth cleared her throat, and leaned closer as well. "I . . . I've been thinking. If we wait until the others are out of camp, in the cave, as they are now or maybe . . . well . . . well—"

"Well, what?" Angie asked.

"Well, maybe one of you could . . . could entertain the one left on guard, and the others could escape—"

"And how far would we get?" Angie snapped. "We'd need several hours' head start to do us the least good."

"And I, for one," Vivian said, a look of disgust on her face, "would not consider 'entertaining' one of those savages . . . not for any reason. My, God, could you imagine carrying the child of one of those men? You'd have a demon in your belly."

"Not even so Cassie could escape?" Marybeth asked.

Vivian sighed deeply, studying her fingers as she ran them through Cassie's silky hair. "Maybe, but only to distract for a moment." Then she looked from Angie to Marybeth. "One of us could get the guard's undivided attention; then while he was becoming busy with what was at hand"—she smiled slightly—"maybe even with his trousers down, one of the other of us could slip up behind, and put a rock to his hard head, well before he spilled his seed."

This time it was Angie's turn to laugh. "I've known men . . . heard of it, of course . . . who spilled their seed just eyeing a willing woman."

"I'd be willing to help any of them spill his brains," Vivian said, and they all smiled at the thought. "It's only three or four more days. We probably should wait and see just how this piece of theater ends . . . farce or tragedy."

"I'd guess the latter," Angie said, her face falling. "It sure ain't been no comedy so far."

"The risk is just too great," Vivian said. "There's only a few days, and then, God willing, we'll be free."

Marybeth broke into tears.

Angie moved over beside her to comfort her. "There, there, child. It'll all be fine."

Sobbing between words, Marybeth finally got out, "It's not . . . it's not all right. It'll never be all right again. Not if I carry a half-breed child."

Vivian was a bit taken aback, then said quietly, "Marybeth, a child is a child, to be treasured, loved, and cared for. Even while it's in your belly. Just pray, if you're with child, that it's healthy and whole."

Chapter 17

But Angie stared at her.

"How . . . how could that be?" Angie asked. "You haven't been out of our sight for more'n the time it took to relieve yourself in the bushes."

"He came to me in the night, put a knife to my throat, then led me outside."

"Who?" Vivian demanded.

"The one who calls himself Badger-Hat."

They were silent for a long while, as Marybeth sobbed quietly.

"Tonight," Vivian said, "you sleep between Angie and me."

"He'll take *you*, Viv," Marybeth said.

"No, he won't. I'll scream and wake the dead."

"He'll kill you."

"Then he'll kill me," Vivian said with finality. She rose, picking Cassie up with her. "Let's go inside and get some rest."

At dawn, Chaco sent Teacher, Tom Badger-Hat, and Crooked-Arm Charley over the ridge in search of the source of the gunfire.

The sun was barely over the mountains to the east when they found Doyle Venton's gray, quietly grazing. They paused long enough to saddle him up and string him out behind with a lead-rope. In a few hundred yards, they found Olaf Pettersen's cold camp, and Doyle Venton, still alive, but barely.

"Who is he?" Badger-Hat asked.

Both the others shrugged as they studied the tracks leaving the camp.

"Don't know," Teacher said, "but he had company. Whoever shot 'im down headed out to the east at a fair pace . . . one walking, one riding."

"How long?" Crooked-Arm Charley asked.

Again, Badger-Hat shrugged. "Maybe last night, maybe saw us come and hightailed after daybreak. We run 'em down?"

"This old boy still has his guns and we got his horse. He ain't going nowhere . . . his back looks like ground meat. Let's get him on his horse and lead him back and see what Chaco wants to do."

"He die on way," Badger-Hat said as they hefted him across his saddle and strapped him down like a sack of flour.

"His horse mine," Crooked-Arm Charley said.

"The hell," Teacher said, eyeing the bigger man and laying his hand on the butt of his revolver as he did.

"Horse mine," Charley said, also resting his hand on the butt of his revolver.

Badger-Hat pushed his horse between them. "Chaco say who gets what. Good rifle, good six-gun, good horse and saddle. Enough for everyone."

"Humph," Teacher said, but gigged his horse on up ahead. "We'll see about this."

When they rode into camp, the women hurried forward and helped drag Venton out of the saddle, and laid him by the fire. They stripped his bloody waistcoat and shirt away.

"His back is full of buckshot," Vivian said. "I'll need a small knife . . . if it's not too deep, I'll get it out."

"He die," Badger-Hat said, and shrugged.

Chaco had walked out of the cave and stood staring down at the man. "Why?" he said.

"Maybe he's worth something," Angie said.

"What he have besides horse?" Chaco asked the three who'd brought him in, and walked over and inspected the gray.

"Winchester and Colt sidearm," Teacher said. "I was first to the horse . . . he should be mine."

"You can have him . . . when I'm through with him. Take weapons in cave. They mine too."

"That horse mine," Badger-Hat said, scowling.

"My blade will be yours, for the time takes to gut you," Chaco said, eyeing him casually.

Badger-Hat spun on his heel and stomped away. Teacher got red in the face, but he made no more claim, nor did the others. Instead, he went looking for his jug and a taste of whiskey.

"A small knife?" Vivian repeated.

Chaco shrugged. "Give it," he said to the others.

Crooked-Arm Charley dug in his pocket and came up with a small folding knife and handed it to her.

She moved over and stuck the blade in the fire, then turned to Angie. "Heat some water and get something for rags. This is going to take a while. . . . I hope he stays unconscious. See if you can make him some broth . . . if he lives long enough to take some."

By the next morning, Venton was sitting up, sipping broth.

* * *

The next day passed uneventfully at the stage station, an off day when the stage wasn't expected.

Killian had decided it was time for him to ride out to find his brother, even though the kin hadn't arrived to help out.

He was at the barn door, saddling his big grulla, and about to heave himself up in the saddle, when he looked back up the wagon road and saw what at first he thought was an Indian, riding one horse, and leading another that was pulling a travois. Then he recognized the big dun, then the buckskin and his brother.

He now loosened the latigo, and let the saddle fall at his feet.

He moved out to the hitching rail in front of the stage station, then seeing how slowly Kane was moving, walked to the door, opened it, and yelled to the kitchen. "Mrs. Pettibone. Kane's on his way down the hill, pulling a travois. Looks like you got a hurt man coming in. Might be fine to have the coffee hot."

Martha Pettibone looked out of the kitchen door, and glared at Kill. "My coffeepot is on the fire, day and night. You help Clarence get those men to the table . . . or the bed. I'll handle things in the kitchen, or the nursin'."

"Yes, ma'am," Kill said, chuckling.

He limped out to the hitching rail, and only had to wait a moment before Kane reined up in front of it.

"Is he dead?" Kill asked, eyeing the substantial load on the travois.

"Times I wish the sumbitch was," Kane said, and brushed himself off, sending billows of dust in the air. "He would be, if Doyle Venton had his way."

"Venton. Figures, Pettersen shot in the back."

"Did you take Venton down?" Kill asked.

"Olaf did. I left him, bleedin' bad, only a rifle shot from Chaco's camp. If they came, they most likely skinned him."

Martha appeared in the doorway. "Can he walk?" she yelled at Kane.

"Doubt it. He's feverish. Been talking to his'sef off and on the last ten miles. Damn if that man can't curse, in two or three languages, I'd imagine."

Martha smiled and nodded, then turned to Kill. "Kill, fetch Clarence. You two'll need help getting Mr. Pettersen inside. I'll go boil up some water and cloth to clean the wound and dress it."

"Yes, ma'am," Kill said, and headed for the barn, leading Kane's buckskin to be rubbed down and grained.

Martha walked outside and leaned over Pettersen, offering him a ladle of water. "You're alive, Mr. Pettersen."

"By God . . . I'm a hard one . . . to kill," the big man mumbled, his voice weak.

Martha turned to Kane, who was unhitching the makeshift drag from the big half-Clydesdale dun. "Kane, you find those heathens and the poor souls with them?"

"I did, and might have gotten home with a couple of the ladies, but they . . . she . . . would have none of it."

"And why the devil not?" Martha asked, a bit indignant.

"Chaco said he'd kill any who remain, one of them tries to escape. It's kinda one for all and all for one, up there in Chaco's camp . . . so far as the prisoners go."

"Well, you get a good night's sleep, and maybe your kin will ride in tomorrow . . . or maybe the next day."

"I'm sleeping five hours, then I'm riding back out."

"Hogwash," Martha said. "You been on the trail for days. Get some real rest—"

Kane handed her a near-empty canvas sack. "I'd appreciate it if you'd fill me up, enough for a week."

"So you're going back out?"

"I am. Soon as my body will oblige."

"May God cup you in the palm of his hand."

"From your lips to God's ears, Martha. Let's get this big bonehead inside."

Kane had slept hard, far longer than he meant to, and it was well after dawn by the time he crawled out of his bedroll in the barn.

He walked out to the corrals behind the barn and relieved himself, then went back through the barn and saw Kill standing beside their horses, both saddled.

Kill looked up as he approached. "Go get Martha to fix you up something. We done et. I'll pack up your bedroll."

"No sign of the McCabes?"

"Nope. If they ride in, they can catch up."

"You sure you're ready to ride?"

"Sure as a whore's heart is hard," Kill said.

"If they're so damn hard, why is it you keep falling in love with them?" Kane said, and laughed.

"I don't never love them for keeping, just for the lovin'. But you're too long in the tooth to understand."

"I believe I understand, although I am not sure I approve. I won't be long."

"Take your time, Grandma." Kane had almost made the door before Kill called out to him. "Whoa. Take a look up the trail. Those ol' boys will be wantin' to grub up and maybe rest up. The kin is here."

"There's three of them," Kane said, shading his eyes from the morning sun, staring at the men pounding the road in the distance.

"Ain't nobody got shoulders that wide, 'cept Cousin Ryan."

"Damned if it ain't. Chaco had better turn tail and head for the high country. It'll be Katy-bar-the-door soon. I'll go ask Martha what she can whip up."

By the time he returned, the McCreeds' second cousins, Dillon and Ethan McCabe and Ryan O'Rourke, had reined up and were dropping from the saddle. By the look of them, and the way the horses were lathered, they'd been in the saddle for most of the night.

They shook hands all around, loosened the cinches on the horses and led them to water, where Clarence took over their care, then headed inside, where Martha was already loading the table with leftovers from the earlier breakfast.

"There'll be fresh biscuits and more bear ham and cackleberries in a while," she called out as she headed for the kitchen. "That's a fine huckleberry jam there . . . big ol' bear chased Clarence up a tree when he was picking them last fall. That's him you're eatin' . . . the bear, not Clarence." She laughed hardily at her own joke. "Make do till I can whip the rest together and put some more life in this gravy."

The men sat around the Pettibones' big table.

"You gonna need some sleep?" Kane asked them.

"We slept a couple of hours last night," Dillon, the oldest of the two, answered, "till the moon came up. We got a few hours left in us. How far we got?"

"It's only twenty-five miles to where these boys are holed up, but it's a hard rough-and-tumble twenty-five, and a fair climb to boot."

Ethan dug right into the bear ham and cold biscuits, and talked while he chewed. "How 'bout we get close, then rest up. When I'm on a hot trail, I'd as soon get close."

Kane nodded. "That's a fine idea. While you're catching some shut-eye, I can reconnoiter their camp. They're due to ride in here for ransom money in three days, and they could be working their way this way. These are hard old boys, and I want the edge on them, not the other way around."

"Who we huntin' and why? Not that it matters much," Dillon said, still eating.

Kane realized he had only said he had a job of work to do, and needed help, in the letter he'd sent. The kin had presumed it was gun work—against a lot of guns—or Kane wouldn't have been asking for help.

Kane smiled. "I guess I could mention why I pried you away from home and hearth. By the way, where'd you dig up this lout?" Kane nodded his head at his cousin Ryan O'Rourke, whom he was surprised to see. "Last I heard he was breaking rocks down Yuma way."

Ryan glanced up from his plate. "While you boys were breaking rocks up Deer Lodge way. Seems jailhouses are the curse of the kin. I left Arizona in a bit of a rush, due to an accident happened to a couple of the guards who'd mistreated me while I was in their care, and decided to take up cattle raising with these two."

"I imagine that accident would be them falling down from carrying too much lead?"

"Something like that," Ryan said, never missing a stroke with his fork.

"Speaking of incarceration," Kane said, "brings me to the why of it. Chaco Sixdog shared a cell with me in Deer Lodge, and killed a fine friend of mine who did him no wrong. I got a letter from Morris Flannigan, head of security for the railroad, who I had some dealings with due to our scuttling that side-wheeler they owned up on the Missouri. Anyways, he posted a ten-thousand-dollar reward for Sixdog, on account of him robbing the train and abducting a half-dozen passengers . . . four of whom he still holds, having killed two of them, a husband and wife."

Kane stared off a little guiltily, then continued. "We take care of Chaco and his bunch, get the rest of the passengers to safety, and collect the ten thousand. Fact is, I'd go after Sixdog no matter the money. He's a blight on the countryside. The sumbitch is hoof-and-mouth, a ten-year dry spell, and a norther with ten feet of snow, all that throwed in together. He is in serious need of killin', as is any man who'd ride with him."

"Well, now," Ethan said, "that's a fair reason for this Sunday ride we been on. I ain't near as sleepy now."

Kane chuckled. "You'll need your rest, bucko, if we're to bring down Chaco Sixdog. This ain't his first go-round. He's mean and tough as a desert sidewinder, stealthy as a puma, and strong as a griz. And a couple of the breeds with him might take him, one on one. I can assure you all, this ain't gonna be a jollification."

Martha walked in with a fresh platter and, while thinking of Chaco Sixdog, they got serious about eating.

When they'd finished the last bite of one of Martha's excellent apple pies, Ethan stood. "I'm gonna have to curl up in the sun like an old hound dog, we don't get to pounding ground."

Kane rose also, stretched, and yawned, and said, "Let's go tack old Chaco's hide to the privy wall."

In minutes, horses grained, watered, and resaddled, the five of them were riding west at a comfortable lope.

Chapter 18

The dust of the kin's horses had hardly settled when four other men reined up at the stage station's hitching rail.

Cheyenne City Marshal Collin Gratsworth, Deputy Marcus McMann, and Deputy Hiram Lavender, who still wore his arm in a sling, were in the company of Morris Flannigan, head of security for the Union Pacific Railroad's Mid-Line Section.

Flannigan's and Gratsworth's saddlebags were stuffed with twenty-dollar gold pieces, fifteen thousand dollars in total. Seven hundred fifty shiny twenty-dollar double-eagle gold pieces, freshly minted earlier in the year in Denver. Each of their four saddlebags carried twelve and a half pounds of gold coin.

Flannigan had decided to carry the gold horseback, rather than on the stage, as the stage had been robbed twice in the last month, and no one would suspect four roughly dressed horsebackers to be carrying a small fortune in gold.

He'd offered Gratsworth and his men the job of guarding his transport, and the marshal had jumped at the chance when he'd been told that Kane McCreed was on the prod for Chaco Sixdog, and that the money was to ransom the road's passengers from that heathen.

Gratsworth still figured that wherever Kane McCreed was, he'd find Killian—and now he wanted them both.

Clarence Pettibone walked out of the barn and laid a pitchfork aside, then came to meet the four men.

"Are the McCreeds about?" Collin asked bluntly, without so much as a hello.

Clarence stopped abruptly and looked from one man to the other, eyeing them carefully. He noted the copper badge on Collin's waistcoat, and only then answered. "You're the law from Cheyenne?"

"That's a question, not an answer," Gratsworth snapped.

"I know the difference, young fella," Clarence said. "Seems you rode in here to my property—"

"This belongs to the stage line—"

"No, I contract with the stage line. This here hundred sixty acres belongs to me, and if you want to take your leave here, and some of my Martha's fine cooking, you'll fix your attitude. All are welcome here, until they make themselves unwelcome, and you've made a good start of it."

Gratsworth reached up and smoothed his chin whiskers and pork-chop sideburns. Then, in a much more friendly tone, and with a tight smile, he said, "We would like to take advantage of your woman's cooking, should the cost be fair."

"Fine, go on inside, with hat in hand. Martha's always pouring hot coffee."

"The McCreeds?" Collin pressed.

"Rode out a while back," Clarence said.

"How long a while and what direction?"

Clarence glared at him for a long moment, obviously

not saying what he was thinking. Then, in a level tone, he said, "I suggest you get in to Martha's table."

Collin eyed him as if he'd like to take a bullwhip to him, but led his deputies inside, without pressing the issue further.

Morris Flannigan stepped forward and extended his hand, introducing himself.

"I've heard a lot about you, Mr. Flannigan," Clarence said. "You're welcome here."

"I'm carrying the ransom money for that robber band. You heard anything more of them?"

"This is for you, not for that marshal?"

"For me," Flannigan said with a serious nod. "No matter Gratsworth's bluster, he's a fine hand with a firearm. Right now, he's hired help to guard this transport, and make sure we get a fair trade when Sixdog comes calling—passengers for the money. So, it's for me and me alone."

"He's twenty-five miles upriver, then up on a high ridge, or so reports Kane McCreed. Kane's going after him now, with the help of some Montana fellas."

"God, I wish I could have gotten to him before they rode out. I don't want this messed up. The railroad wants to pay Sixdog the money, get the passengers back, then run him down later. Kane could mess that all up."

Clarence shrugged. "Kane don't light long in one place. He said it was you who suggested he run Chaco down. In fact, a ten-thousand-dollar reward and the phrase 'Bring me Chaco's head'—does that mean anything to you?"

"That was before I heard from the powers that be in Omaha. I got people to answer to. I guess all we can do is sit tight and wait."

"Guess so," Clarence said, but eyed him with some

suspicion. He'd sent Kane after Sixdog, and now he awaited him with three lawmen who wanted a piece of Kane's hide, or worse.

Clarence had had many dealings with the railroad, and had learned not to trust them. In fact, trusting them was a little like thinking a timber rattler would like you to stand on his tail. And it looked to Clarence like the road was giving good reason for distrust one more time.

He followed the four inside, just in time to hear Gratsworth call out, "Woman, get some lunch in here."

Clarence crossed the room to stand across the table from Gratsworth, and eye him for a moment to calm the heat in his backbone. Then he spoke, carefully but emphatically. "Marshal, my missus goes by Mrs. Pettibone, and she'll be happy to set a fine table for you. Howsome-ever, your fifty cents will not make nor break this stage station. You yell at her again, and I will personally pour her hot coffeepot in your lap."

Morris Flannigan's laugh interrupted Collin's red-faced reply. "Collin, I'd like to eat, and would appreciate it if you'd not tempt Mrs. Pettibone to put lye in the beans. Let me do the talking from now on. Understand?"

Gratsworth sat back in his chair, clamping his jaw so tightly the veins showed in his neck.

Chaco waved Teacher over, and motioned for him to sit on a rock next to him.

"We pack up and head out," Chaco said.

"We ain't supposed to be at Greybull till day after tomorrow."

"No matter. White men too close. We ride out, then we spend some time watching stage station before we ride in for money."

"And the women?"

"They stay back in the trees with Badger-Hat and Black Eagle."

"I don't trust Badger-Hat."

"It not for you to say. They stay, you, me, and Charley ride in for money—after make sure not a trap."

"How about that fella, Venton?"

"I talk with him a little. I have heard he a fine gunhand."

Teacher looked skeptical. "Well, he shot some fellas down. But I ain't sure that makes him a hand."

"He ride with us, or die here."

"Then while you're making up your mind, I'm gonna get the boys and pack up. I'm out of whiskey, and it's gnawing at me." Teacher rose and crossed the clearing to where the women and child sat. "Y'all get your things together. We're riding out."

"Good," Angela said without comment. They'd all been waiting for this moment, when they'd be on their way to freedom—God, the railroad, and Chaco Sixdog willing.

The kin rode for four hours before they took a break to water and wind the horses.

Dillon and Ryan reined up beside Kane and they all dismounted.

"How much more?" Dillon asked.

"We're halfway, but the next half is the steep one. Nothing more than a fast walk after another mile or so."

Ryan stretched and yawned. "I'm about beat down to a pasture patty. Any reason we don't camp here and get caught up on the shut-eye?"

"Kane?" Dillon asked.

Kane thought a moment, staring off toward the

distant divide. "Fact is, I think Killian is about wore out—as you can tell by the gimp, he's nursing a bent knee. Why don't you all hold up here, and I'll push hard and try to get a look at their camp before sundown, then let ol' Charger here find his way back while I sleep in the saddle."

"You watch your back trail," Dillon said.

"Don't shoot me when I come into camp—a little after midnight, God willin' and the creek don't rise."

"We'll leave the beans on the fire."

"And your Winchesters at hand. Could be, I'll come back with heathens on my heels."

"Come a-shoutin'," Dillon said with a grin. "I don't wake up as easy as I used to."

"Have no fear of that," Kane said, and gigged the buckskin into a lope out of camp.

"Where's he going?" Killian said, limping up beside them.

"To take a look-see at Chaco's camp."

"Damn, I should be with him." Kill headed for his horse.

"Hey, there, cousin," Dillon said, stopping Kill short.

"What?"

"Kane said you were to wait for him to get back. You're gonna rest that knee."

"The hell. I ain't the whelp of either of you."

Dillon, Ethan, and Ryan gathered around Kill, staring him down, until Dillon finally spoke up. "Kane said wait—your knee says wait. None of us want to nurse-maid you, should we get into it, and Kane assures us we will. Now, if you don't want your kin to give the other knee a twist, you'll settle down on your bedroll."

Kill threw his hat in the dust and sputtered as he

stomped, then limped, away, to drop the saddle from his big grulla.

It took Kane another four hours to reach the draw where Olaf and Doyle Venton had traded shots, and to discover that there was no sign of Venton's body. In another hour, just an hour before sunset, he was looking down a steep ravine at Chaco's camp and the mouth of the cave.

His stomach twisted when he realized no one occupied the camp, and no smoke came from the cave. He pulled the Winchester from the saddle scabbard, then went ahead and let the buckskin pick his way down the slope, tying him in the brush a hundred feet from the cold camp.

It took him only moments to determine that they'd all ridden out, due east, down a canyon and watershed that would take them south of the Greybull drainage.

Chaco was nothing if not smart, and he wouldn't retrace his trail going to a place half the country knew he would be heading. That didn't surprise Kane, but he was angry at himself for waiting to sleep before he'd ridden back out to get to Vivian and the women. Now Chaco was on the trail, and he and his men would be no more than a horse's length away from the women at any one time—and Kane had to find them before he even worried about how to get them away from the Indians.

Damn it.

There would be no sleeping in the saddle while he returned for the others. And little rest for them, if he had anything to say about it.

He gigged the buckskin hard and set him into a gallop. It would be downslope most of the way back to camp, and he intended to take advantage of it until dark forced him to slow the pace.

It was a little before ten o'clock when he rode into camp, shouting as he came so he wouldn't be greeted with a shower of lead.

Dillon sat up in his bedroll. "What the hell you doing back so soon?"

Kane spoke without dismounting. "Camp's empty, they headed down the drainage to the south. Let's get saddled up and see if we can run 'em down."

Chapter 19

Dillon shook his head, trying to clear the sleep, then asked Kane, "You want to ride dark and maybe stumble into a camp full of hard men bent on cuttin' you down?"

"What do you have in mind?"

"If you know they're headed back to Greybull Station, then let's set up somewhere twixt them and it, and wait."

Kane thought for a moment, then dismounted and walked over to his brother. "Kill, you remember that deep canyon we came through, about five miles south of the station?"

"Yeah. Creek runs right alongside the road."

"Good place for an ambush?"

"Good as any."

"Good, lead the boys there."

"Where're you going?"

"I'm gonna find 'em, and dog their trail, just to make sure we know what they're about. Chaco is too smart to ride into a trap, and he don't know half the damn Union Army ain't waiting for him. He'll spread his forces. I don't want them hiding the women out somewhere where we can't find them, and the only way to be sure of that is to know exactly what they're doing."

Kill rose to his feet and stretched. "These ol' boys can find their way there. Hell, it's on the road. I'm riding with you."

"Damn the flies, Kill. You're dinged up and I ain't gonna spend time worrying about you—"

"When did you ever have to—"

"When I had to pluck you out of that tree, like a fat old partridge, and about a score of other times. You're staying with Dillon, Ryan, and Ethan. I'm going alone. A'sides, I'll need to ride quiet, and one is more quiet than two ever'time."

"Damn it—"

"That's the way it is, Kill. You'll get your bellyful afore this is over. I'm pounding trail."

Dillon put a hand on Killian's shoulder. "We need you to show the way, Kill." Then he turned to Kane. "We'll get some more shut-eye, then ride out a couple of hours before sunup. If they camped, and there's no reason to think they didn't, we'll be at your canyon well before they come moseyin' along. Keep your head down."

Kane swung back up in the saddle.

"You want to ride the grulla?" Kill asked. "He's fresh."

"I'm gonna cross the ridge and get a few miles south, then wait till there's some light on things. We'll have three or four hours to rest up."

With that, he spun the buckskin and started south, climbing up through scattered chaparral and lodgepole pine to the ridge above.

Doyle Venton had convinced Chaco that he was nothing but a traveling man, who'd been shot down by a bandit. Although he had nothing but his clothes, horse, and tack, he had friends and those friends would pay for his safe return. It was a lie, but it kept him alive. He was placed on the worst of the band's horses, a bandy-legged piebald, and forced to ride with his wrists bound, ahead of the women.

Vivian was riding with Cassie in the saddle in front of her; tied to their saddle was a lead-rope from Angie Bolander's horse, and in turn a lead-rope was tied from her animal leading that of Marybeth Pettersen's. A pair of the Indians rode behind them, leading packhorses, and Chaco, Teacher, and Black Eagle rode ahead. Crooked-Arm Charley was scouting far ahead, watching for signs of an ambush. Occasionally, Chaco would send Teacher or Black Eagle up the slopes on either flank to scout for trouble.

Venton had considered trying to give heels to the horse, but the animal was just not fit enough to outrun those of the Indians, and he was still not fit himself, as the wounds in his back continued to weep. Instead, he decided to bide his time and stay alive.

Vivian was growing closer and closer to the precious little girl, and although she regretted not being able to try and escape with Kane McCreed, she would make the same decision, had she had it to do over. She wouldn't leave the other women, and she certainly wouldn't leave Cassie.

But she was frightened. She had a terrible foreboding that though they were this close to freedom, even having Chaco Sixdog tell them that they'd soon be free, something terrible was yet to happen.

She prayed not—but that didn't quell the butterflies in her stomach.

One more night . . . please God, let there only be one

more night with these savages. So far, both her honor and her life had been spared, but the looks Chaco continued to give her said her honor wouldn't be spared long.

She hoped and prayed tomorrow would see the end of her imprisonment.

They rode for six hours; then Chaco moved into a grove of tall cottonwoods, rimmed by a thick stand of chokecherries. A small creek that had started out a mere pace wide was now four paces wide, and had continually been widening as they'd moved down the long canyon, and the hills flanking the creek were now low, crowned with only the occasional stand of pines. They'd just seen their first herd of antelope; Vivian knew they were nearing the high plains.

They dismounted, and Chaco sent the women to collect firewood while the men unsaddled and unloaded the packhorses.

One more night.

Kane had ridden over the high rise and down a long cleft in the mountains until he'd reached the valley floor. Then he'd watered the buckskin at a trickle, reined him into a deep dark stand of ponderosa, dropped the saddle from the big horse, and staked him with a picket pin to a long tether.

He'd slept for four hours, he figured by the movement of the stars, when he was up again saddling the horse. When they'd moved down out of the stand of trees, he kept the horse at a brisk walk, and finally, when the sun began to make silhouettes of the trees on the mountaintops ahead, moved him into a lope.

Keeping a sharp eye, he continually scanned the area

ahead, desperate to find Viv and Chaco's camp, but
wary that he'd ride into a waking camp full of men
armed to the teeth and chomping at the bit to take his
hair for saddle folderol.

When it got light enough, he could make out the trail
of what seemed a dozen horses; then as he got lower in
elevation, and the ponderosa on the slopes became
stands of lodgepole and then were peppered with decid-
uous trees, and finally the bottom of the canyon became
a wide stream lined with cottonwood, he slowed.

In the harsh light of mid-morning he was on their
camp, almost before he knew it, but luckily, they'd
ridden out. By the feel of their small campfire, he figured they'd been gone less than an hour, maybe only a
half hour.

The hillsides were now broken with groves of trees
bordering broad meadows, and some of the wheatgrass
and wild oat meadows extended over the tops of the
rolling hills. He moved upslope, away from the major
game trail they were following in the canyon bottom,
and kept to the top of the ridge. He could be skylined
there on the top, but not severely until later in the day,
and he knew he was close to them and didn't want to
stumble on them.

Finally, he spotted a wisp of dust, and dropped down
a ways until he was below the ridgeline. The going was
tougher there, as he had to pick his way through the occasional copse of trees, but finally he caught sight of
them. He waited until they were out of sight, then rode
hard, up and over the ridgeline, and set the big buckskin
into a hard gallop, down the valley, but out of sight of
the band over the ridgetop.

He pounded at a gallop, until the buckskin was
winded. Then he reined up and let him rest, dropping

his reins in the middle of a patch of grass, while he moved, on foot, up to the top of the ridge to position himself in an outcropping of rocks. He lay quietly, over a quarter mile above the bottom of what had been a canyon, but was now a deep-dish swale. His wait was rewarded as they rode into sight.

He wished he had a pair of the Army's high-dollar binoculars, but he didn't. Sure that there were nine of them, if he'd counted all when he had studied their camp before, he was comfortable to again count nine. Plus one of the women seemed to have something on the saddle in front of her. He presumed that was the little girl.

Making out the fact that three of the nine riders were women, he thought that the one riding with the child in the saddle in front of her was Vivian—but he couldn't be sure.

And he had to be sure.

He'd started to try and slip down the face of the hillside to get closer, when he suddenly heard the clink of horseshoes on rock. Dropping deep in the cleft of the rocks, he slipped the Bland-Pryce from its holster and cradled it in hand. A couple more clanks of horseshoe on rock, then the steady clomp, clomp of a walking horse. He was afraid to rise up, afraid that he and the rider would see each other at the same time, as the sound was close. He would have the drop on the rider, but if he was forced to fire, he would alert those below. So he hunkered low and waited, as a black raven circled overhead, cawing loudly, warning all of his presence.

Suddenly, the man rode into sight, his upper torso showing above the level of the rock over which Kane looked.

If he glanced over. . . .

But the raven cawed loudly, just as the man passed, and the man looked up and studied the raven.

Kane smiled tightly as he'd misjudged the raven, who'd saved him from being seen.

Kane only then realized the dirty, gray-bearded, buckskin-clad man was not Indian, but white. He must be the man who was with Chaco at the stage stop—the man Clarence Pettibone had called Teacher—when Chaco delivered the ransom note, the man who Kane figured had written the note.

But the man didn't look over. He passed on by, and Kane let out a long breath, realizing that he'd been holding it, and eased his grip on the Bland-Pryce's trigger.

That was too close, he thought as the sound of hooves faded.

He waited until the man had time to get fifty yards along the hillside, then rose just enough that his eye line was over the rock top.

So there were ten of them, including the women, plus the little girl. The thought came to him that one of them might be Doyle Venton, if Venton had lived. It would be like Venton, Kane guessed, to take up with a filthy band like those Chaco led.

Kane relaxed back into the cleft for a while, then rose, checked to see that his enemies were out of sight, and sprinted back over the rise to where he'd staked the buckskin. In moments, he was pounding back down the slope where he figured he'd be out of sight of the bearded man, even if he topped the rise to check the valley on the other side of the ridge.

He galloped hard, wanting to get well ahead of the gang, so this time he could get hidden close enough to the trail in the bottom of the swale that he could see for absolute surity exactly who the riders were—and that Vivian was safe among them, at least for the time being.

He followed at a distance, but the country continued to open up, and it would be more and more difficult to close on the band without being seen. He'd wait until they made camp, then close on them in the dark as he had before.

And he did.

As Chaco turned north from his easterly trek, Kane paralleled the road, a mile or two east of their path, and was satisfied that they were heading for the stage station, and the money.

Now, the question was, where would Chaco hole up with the women? Where would he leave them, so if he rode into an ambush at the stage station and escaped, he would still have his hostages?

There was no question in Kane's mind that Chaco would leave them. And there was no question that Chaco would have to drop down into the canyon that held the road in order to make the last few miles to the stage station—the canyon where the kin awaited. The ambush that would, should, surprise Chaco, as it would be well before where he expected.

Kane stayed a mile behind the band, waiting with a hunter's patience.

It wasn't long before his wait was rewarded.

Chapter 20

After they'd reached the road in late afternoon, and stayed north along it for two miles, nearing the canyon where Kane hoped the kin awaited, Chaco swung back west, climbing a steep slope up into the tree line. Behind it, there was a cleft in the cliff face, and far above, a steep rocky-shouldered mountain.

Kane followed, but kept to the south where he could make his way through a stand of lodgepole and aspens. As he surmised, they were about to make camp. He followed carefully, moving very slowly, letting the buckskin graze. When he neared the rocky slopes of the mountain without seeing where they'd gone, he dismounted and staked the horse in a grassy portion of the meadow that intruded into the trees, where the animal could easily reach a trickle of water that seeped from the rock face.

He could see a cleft in the cliff face, and presumed that they must have found a way up out of the meadow, via that steep walled arroyo.

Knowing that they wouldn't go far in the oncoming darkness in such tough country, Kane bided his time. He wasn't about to follow them into the arroyo, where he could be easily picked off by a camp guard. While he waited, he studied the cliff wall. There appeared to be plenty of handholds to climb up to where he might locate Chaco's camp, but the way down, in the dark, would be pure hell.

He could merely wait, hoping they came back the way they'd gone, retracing their tracks back down to the road. But what if there was another way out? He could lose them totally, and if they circled the canyon where the kin awaited, what then?

No, he had to make the climb, four hundred feet, he estimated, and risk the return in the dark.

Just at twilight, his reata draped over his shoulder, he began to ascend the face, following a cleft that would take him halfway up, climbing easily. But then he ran out of cleft, and handholds.

If his eyes had served him, the going was easier slightly to the south of where the cleft ended, where the occasional brush, and even a tenacious pine or two, grew from the face of the rock wall. His reata was sixty-five feet long, which meant he could double it, tying a slipknot around the base of one of the thicker stumps of brush, and if he fell, it would allow a bone-breaking fall, but would stop him from tumbling two hundred or more feet to the base of the cliff, which would likely kill him. The slipknot would allow him to pull on one tail of the reata, and free the knot below, allowing him to repeat the process.

After taking a turn around his waist, around the stump of brush, and holding the tail of the slipknot, he could move up only twenty feet before he had to pull the knot, fight the reata free of the brush, and find another stump. After the third such climb, he was facing true darkness, and thought he was still fifty or sixty feet from the top, where a line of pines signified a true flat, that was at least a ledge, if not a wide step in the mountain.

Just in the last rays of twilight, he spotted a rock outcropping, no more than twenty feet above him. He formed a loop, and on the third try, managed to lasso the outcropping. He tested his weight on the rock, and it seemed solid. If it gave way, with his reata now used to climb with, there was nothing between him and a hundred-fifty-foot fall from which he'd never awake.

Pulling himself hand over hand, his feet catching whatever edge they could, he was just about to grasp the rock that had caught his loop, when he felt it begin to give. He lunged for the edge, and caught it just as the rock broke free, and sailed out into space.

Then he realized he still had a firm hold on the reata, its tail under his grasping hand, its loop still around the falling rock. He was able to relocate his grip, just as it was ripped away, taking some skin off his palm with it—but it didn't wrench him free of his precarious hold. His gut was knotted as tight as the muscles in his shoulders, when he realized how close he'd come to being ground meat and shattered bones at the cliff bottom.

He caught his breath, and with a giant heave, pulled himself up to where he could get a leg up, and finally his body to rest on the ledge. Not yet at the top, he collapsed in a heap, and rested. If starlight served him, the rest of the way was merely a hand-over-hand-pray-for-foothold climb.

When finally well rested, and with the snakes in his belly calmed, he worked his way on up the tree line, and then through a gentle climb until he broke out into a meadow. He could hear a trickle of water that was probably the beginning of the same stream that served Charger, his buckskin, at the bottom of the cliff face.

He paused, listening to the sound of the water, then made his way toward it, until he was at the trickle's edge. Kneeling, he washed the burn in his palm, then filled his hands and drank, then drank again, realizing how the climb had winded him and dried his gullet.

Then he heard the sound of laughter, then a loud guffaw, that echoed down through the trees.

Chaco's camp was close, no more than a hundred yards through the trees at most.

He now moved like a very cautious hunter—three steps, then wait and listen, then three more. Closing what he felt was half the distance, he dropped to his hands and knees, and moved through the heavy brush until he could make out the glow of a low campfire. Again, he heard men talking, mostly in a language he didn't comprehend.

Confident that the guard's outpost would be somewhere below where he could watch the deep arroyo, Kane inched forward.

He froze at the sound of a stream of water, realizing that someone was very close, urinating, just out of eyesight of the camp. He heard the man sigh, hack, spit, then move away.

Finally, he could make out the camp, forty yards away through the underbrush, and saw that they'd built the fire backed by a ledge, in a wind hollow of the rock face.

The fire was so low, he couldn't make out faces.

He inched forward another ten yards, then clearly heard the crystal-clear voice of Vivian, as she sung a lullaby to the child, and he could see her, rocking and holding the little girl in her arms.

Satisfied, Kane backed away, slowly, until he was more than sixty yards from the camp; then he turned and moved quickly back to the edge of the cliff.

He eyed it for a long time, then decided that he could do Viv no good if he was a pile at the bottom of the cliff. Moving deep into the tree line, he found a spot and curled up to spend a cold night, deciding the wise thing to do was to wait until they rode out in the morning, then take the much easier arroyo back down to the canyon bottom, following in their tracks, recovering Charger, and then catching up with them.

Killian McCreed, Dillon and Ethan McCabe, and Ryan O'Rourke had arisen early and saddled and ridden out, retracing their steps back toward the Greybull Stage Station. As the trail joined the road almost three miles south of the stage station, Dillon did not want to waste time by covering the six miles out of the way it would require to ride to the station, yet he did want to make sure Chaco had not ridden hard and circled them.

He sent young Ethan, while the rest of them turned south to reach the narrows where they'd set up their ambush and hoped to rescue the passengers and take down the half-breed, Chaco, who Dillon looked upon as a meal ticket.

Ethan loped the three miles to Greybull, passing the down-line stage, on its way to Rockville, and waving as he did so. The whip driving and the shotgun guard gave him a wave in return, and the guard continued to eye him carefully, while the whip concentrated on the team.

When Ethan reined up in front of the station, Clarence was still stripping harness from the well-lathered six-up. Ethan crossed the yard to help him, just as Marshal

Collin Gratsworth walked out of the building, his Winchester hanging casually in hand.

"Hey!" Gratsworth yelled at him.

Ethan turned and eyed the man, seeing the copper badge on his waistcoat. "Hey what?" Ethan asked.

"You come in from the south?"

"Why do you ask?" Ethan said, not much liking the man's manner.

"I'm the law, just answer the question."

Ethan walked back to face him, the marshal still standing on the elevated porch in front of the station. Ethan looked him up and down, and leaned closer to read the badge.

"City Marshal, it says."

"I know what it says," Gratsworth snapped.

"Don't say Greybull Stage Station, Marshal," Ethan said, a lazy smile crossing his face.

"I know what it says. It says I'm the law."

"You might be the law somewheres, but this is Greybull, and Greybull doesn't have any law, unless you'd be a federal marshal?"

"I'm city marshal of Cheyenne, and I asked you a question." Gratsworth slowly edged the muzzle of the Winchester so it pointed at Ethan's stomach.

Clarence saw the growing confrontation, and he was already tired to the bone of Collin Gratsworth. He dropped the armful of collars he was carrying, and closed the distance between the team and the porch.

Ethan spoke very carefully. "You might be a little careful where you aim that thing, Marshal. I don't take kindly to having some fool shoot me by mistake."

"I ain't no fool. What about a'purpose?" Gratsworth asked, then clamped his jaw and raised the muzzle to heart height. "The sun shall not smite thee by day, nor

the moon by night, says the Bible, but it don't say nothing about me smiting you whenever and wherever I
damn well please. I am the law."

"Gratsworth!" Clarence yelled as he was within ten
feet of the two men.

The marshal turned his eyes to the hostler, and swung
the muzzle slightly away from Ethan as he did so.

Ethan took a half step forward, grabbed the muzzle,
and jerked the rifle with both hands, its muzzle pointed
off to the side. Gratsworth tried to hang on, but was
jerked sprawling off the porch into the dust and onto his
back at Ethan's feet. In a heartbeat, Ethan had the
muzzle of the rifle pressed into the marshal's chest, and
was smiling at him.

"Now, Marshal, was there something you wanted to
know 'bout where I been or where I'm going?"

Gratsworth, fire in his eyes, tried to reach for his
sidearm, but Ethan stomped his wrist hard, and he
jerked the hand away. He tried to rise, but Ethan shoved
the muzzle into his breastbone, pushing him back down.

"You're assaultin' the law," Gratsworth sputtered.

"I'm not in Cheyenne, Marshal, don't ya know."
Ethan was still smiling.

"What the hell . . ." It was one of Gratsworth's
deputies, standing in the doorway. He pulled his revolver, and leveled it at Ethan's wide back.

Chapter 21

Clarence stepped in between them, just as the deputy cocked the revolver, blocking the deputy's view. "I'll have none of this. You four are about to wear out your welcome."

Clarence started up on the porch, just as Morris Flannigan pushed the deputy in the doorway aside, telling him to holster his weapon. "Damned if you three ain't trouble on the hoof," Flannigan muttered, then walked on out and brushed past Clarence, to stand and face Ethan and the still-sputtering Gratsworth. He eyed the situation, then centered hard eyes on Ethan.

"What's the trouble here?" Flannigan asked.

Ethan shrugged. "Not much trouble here. This fella with the pork-chop sideburns let his rifle wander a mite, till it was pointed my way. My old pappy taught me never to point your firearm at something you don't mean to kill, and I'm just trying to make the point here with Mister—what did you say your name was, Marshal?"

Gratsworth could only sputter.

"His name is Marshal Collin Gratsworth, young fella. And who, sir, might you be?"

"Why, I'm Ethan McCabe, now that someone asked in a civil manner."

"You related to Dillon McCabe?" Flannigan asked, then added, "And his cousin Kane McCreed?"

"I am, and proud of it."

"Kane's a fri—an acquaintance of mine. Let the marshal get up."

Ethan eyed him.

"Please," Flannigan said.

Ethan shrugged, but stepped back, still eyeing Gratsworth. "Did you learn my daddy's lesson?" Ethan asked, but got no answer as Gratsworth scrambled to his feet. As the marshal was in a much better position to draw, Ethan cocked the Winchester, but kept the muzzle pointed at the sky.

Gratsworth still had fire in his eyes, but Flannigan reached over, grabbed him by the shoulder, and pushed him toward the station door where the other two deputies stood, watching, but keeping their hands off their weapons.

"Go on inside," Flannigan snapped, "and get yourself a cup of coffee while I chat with this young fella. Seems you can't get along with nobody."

Gratsworth stomped up on the porch and shoved the two deputies out of the way getting inside.

"You riding with Kane?" Morris asked.

Ethan ignored him, turning to Clarence. "Mr. Pettibone, you need help putting that team away?" he asked.

"I wouldn't turn it down, young fella," Clarence said, and started back to his chore, with Ethan on his heels.

Flannigan followed, then repeated the question as Ethan leaned Gratsworth's rifle against a fence rail and set to gathering up the traces and harness. "You ridin' with Kane?"

"I never saw such a talkative bunch as hang out at this stage station," Ethan said as Flannigan followed him into the barn. "What if I am?" he finally asked.

"I got instructions for Kane."

"I might stumble across him," Ethan said. "And should I, I'd be pleased to pass your message along. Kane don't take much to instructions, how-some-ever."

"Fine. You tell him that Morris Flannigan said to leave Chaco Sixdog be. The railroad wants him to ride into this stage station, fancy free, hand over his prisoners—"

"Your passengers," Ethan corrected. "That y'all let get took right off'n your train."

"Our passengers," Flannigan concurred, but reddened slightly. "And ride out with the money. We'll send a posse after him, after the passengers are in my safekeeping."

"Safe—like they were on your train," Ethan said, and grinned, but then turned serious. "I'll pass your message along, but my cousin Kane seems to march to his own drummer, and I wouldn't hang my hat on that peg till Kane's here to agree."

"I'm rescinding the offer of a reward."

Ethan shrugged. "Renegin', you mean. You'll have to take that up with Kane."

"Tell him," Flannigan said, reddening deeply this time.

"That I can do, sir," Ethan answered in a level tone, as Flannigan spun on his heel and headed back to the stage station.

"Where you headed, young fella?" Clarence asked, putting away the last of the tack.

"Back south, to join up with the kin, who are waiting for this fella Chaco to show his ugly mug, notwithstanding what Mr. Flannigan might wish. It seems it's personal business with Kane."

"I overheard Gratsworth plottin' with those deputies. They're laying for Kane and Killian, and Flannigan's not discouraging them. You might let your kin know."

"I will, and I thank you, Mr. Pettibone. But I'd guess Kane won't ride a gnat's-pecker length out of his way to avoid those ol' boys. In fact, the minute I tell him they're looking for him, he'll want to ride right into their face, stare 'em down, and see if they want to put their lead where their mouth is."

Clarence chuckled. "That's the same Kane I know. Do me a favor, and ask him to ride into their face someplace other than Greybull. I've dodged enough lead to last me a lifetime."

"I'll ask him, and try to convince him." Then Ethan grinned broadly. "I'd do a mite better job should you folks would favor me with a bowl of Mrs. Pettibone's cobbler afore I ride out?"

"She just made a fresh one. If you'll wait right here, and not go inside where there's liable to be more trouble, I'll bring out the whole dang cobbler."

"And I'll tote it back to the others, if'n there's some way to carry it?" Ethan asked, plopping down on a stack of sacked rolled oats.

"I'll figure a way. You sit tight," Pettibone said, and hurried away.

While Kane neared Chaco's camp, Ethan rode into the deep canyon where he hoped the kin were holed up, awaiting Chaco and his men. The canyon rose steeply on either side, rugged with rock outcroppings and only the occasional tenacious tree hanging on the rock walls or among boulders on the rock escarpment.

The two-track road in the canyon bottom, used twice

a week by the stage, crossed and recrossed the trickle of a stream that occasionally became a torrent when the thunderclouds crackled and snapped and caused the stage to have to wait outside the canyon mouth until the water receded.

Ethan clomped up the trail, seeing no sign of his brother or cousins, until a voice rang out behind him. "You'd be easy pickin's, brother."

Ethan reined up and looked back over his shoulder, where Dillon stood on a rock, smiling.

As Ethan spoke, Ryan and Kill appeared from behind a rock and tree. "You don't think they'll be along tonight?" Ethan asked.

"Nope, but we need to be ready should they."

"Any sign of Kane?" Ethan asked.

"None."

"You don't suppose Sixdog and his pack got their hands on Cousin Kane?"

"He'll be along," Killian said, limping down the rocky hillside. "I'd guess he's on their tail. Nonetheless, we'll be waiting right here for Sixdog, as agreed."

"No fire?" Ethan asked.

"No fire," Dillon said.

"Then you won't have no coffee to go with the apple cobbler I got in my saddlebags."

Dillon smiled tightly, then said, "I guess a wee fire would do no harm."

Ethan laughed, and dismounted, and the rest of them gathered round.

As the eastern sky began to redden, Kane was already positioned where he could see into the arroyo. He was not surprised to see two of the Indians ride out well ahead of the others, scouts, he presumed, that Chaco would send ahead to make sure no ambush awaited. One of the Indians had a crooked arm; the other wore a dangling pair of dark eagle feathers. Kane let them pass, staying deep in a cleft.

It was almost an hour before the other riders appeared in the distance, their horses carefully picking their way down the steep arroyo.

Kane stayed deep in the shadows of a rock outcropping. The shaggy-bearded white man, who Pettibone had said was called Teacher, was in the lead, with another Indian behind him.

Kane's stomach tightened when he saw Viv, the child in the saddle in front of her, and two women following, their horses tied together and being led by the Indian riding in the second position. Then Kane's stomach knotted when he saw the thick strong torso of Chaco Sixdog, riding directly behind the ladies. Behind him rode Doyle Venton, his hands tied to the saddle horn, the reins tied together fairly tightly over the ugly piebald's neck, and behind him, another Indian.

Kane was a little surprised, and disappointed, that Sixdog had not left the passengers in camp with only a couple of guards. Had he done so, Kane had made up his mind to pick them off, and rescue the women and child right there. But right now, first thing was to get Vivian cut out of the herd; then, and only then, would he go after Sixdog.

He let them get ten minutes in front of him, before he scrambled down to the bottom of the arroyo and trotted to the canyon bottom, then back up the trail to where he'd staked Charger in the tree line. But first, he had to recover his reata, which he found at the cliff face. He was well winded by the time he found the buckskin, but didn't tarry. Quickly saddling the horse, he fell in behind the riders.

He wanted to be right on their heels when the Indians fell under the guns of his waiting kin, close enough that he might pick off any who were successful at a retreat. And more importantly, close enough to make sure Viv was safe. Four, maybe five miles to the canyon, Kane figured, looking ahead where a lemon yellow sun made the mountains that held the rock canyon glow in the morning light.

It would be a fine day, Kane thought. *If I get Viv safely in hand and out of harm's way.*

As they neared the canyon, Kane began to close the distance.

Kill, Dillon, Ryan, and Ethan were well spaced in the canyon, Kill and Dillon on the east side, forty yards up the steep slope and more than forty yards apart, Ryan and Ethan across from them.

They'd argued whether Ryan or Dillon was the best shot, and they had flipped a coin to see who would fire the first shot, and signal the shooting. Ryan O'Rourke had won. He took a position as the northernmost of them, and they'd agreed to let the riders get sandwiched between them before he fired, and, hopefully, the first riders to fall would be those flanking the prisoners, should the prisoners be lined out in the middle of their captors.

Ryan didn't like the fact they'd had to hide the horses in a side canyon, almost a hundred yards up a narrow cut in order to make sure they were out of sight. But it had to be.

Ryan was perplexed when they sunk back into the

shadows at the sight of oncoming riders—because there were only two, and no prisoners rode with them.

Afraid to fire, afraid that he'd alert the other Indians who must be well behind with the prisoners, Ryan slunk back in the shadows and let the men pass.

Morris Flannigan had decided to remain at the stage station alone with the money. He wanted nothing to spook Sixdog, and wanted the transfer to go smoothly. He beseeched Clarence Pettibone to take his wife and ride up the mountain, well away from the coming meeting with Sixdog, the tendering of the money and delivery of the passengers . . . and possible trouble.

Clarence had conceded, as no stage was due, agreeing to stay away for the rest of the afternoon. Olaf Pettersen, feverish and unable to care for himself, was on a pad near the fire in the dining area of the stage stop, and Clarence made Flannigan swear he'd look after him until they returned.

The Pettibones saddled riding horses, and left to hopefully knock down a deer, elk, or antelope for the larder.

Then Flannigan sent the two deputies up opposite hillsides flanking the stage station, with instructions to lay low unless trouble arose. If it did, they'd have a clear field of fire back down at the stage station.

He instructed Collin Gratsworth to ride south on the road a mile or so and find a good spot where he could see well down the approach, and when he saw Sixdog coming, he was to hightail it back to the stage station, give the alarm, then take up a position in the hay storage on the barn's second level, which faced the house and also had a clear field of fire.

Gratsworth was not happy with the plan, but finally

conceded and rode off up the long climb south out of Greybull Canyon.

Morris Flannigan, wanting to appear as unconcerned as if he were sitting on the porch of the Territorial Capital, lit up his pipe and settled into one of Clarence Pettibone's two rocking chairs, the money all in one pair of saddlebags next to him.

It was an hour and a half after they'd taken up their positions on the canyon wall when Ethan, situated so he could see down the road, spotted riders in the distance, and as agreed, gave a low whistle imitating a meadowlark.

They huddled in absolute silence; only the sound of songbirds enjoying the morning could be heard in the canyon bottom, as well as the sound of hoofbeats.

With luck, in minutes, the hostages would be free, and they'd have Chaco's head.

Chapter 22

Ethan was surprised to see Chaco rein up, a good long rifle shot from where he waited. The Indian leader waved one of the other Indians up to palaver with him, then the man took the lead-rope from Chaco, and moved away, starting to take a small canyon to the side. The man with the shaggy beard spurred his horse up alongside Sixdog, and the Indian that had been following reined away to follow the passengers. Ethan studied the group. Sixdog and a gray-bearded white man remained in the trail, while one Indian led three white women, one with a child in the saddle in front of her, and a white man with his hands tied.

It looked as if it would only be Sixdog and the white man, Teacher, who would ride on toward Greybull Stage Station, and under the kin's rifles.

But even before Sixdog could spur up his horse, shots echoed up the canyon.

Collin Gratsworth had set his horse into an easy lope, and had been shocked when a small turn in the trail brought him face-to-face with a pair of Indians. He grabbed his rifle up out of his saddle scabbard, and the Indians followed suit. Gratsworth's shots went wild, as his animal began to buck and pitch.

Black Eagle's trail-wise pony stayed calm, and his first shot took Collin Gratsworth through the throat. Gratsworth's horse, more from instinct than from being reined, spun and started down the trail at a gallop.

The Indians too swung their mounts, and gave them their heels, and in a heartbeat were pounding back up the trail the way they'd come.

Ethan, seeing Chaco and the bearded white man sitting quietly in the trail, watching to see what might come, could stand it no longer, and just as the hostages and two Indians disappeared into the side canyon, leveled down on the men in the trail and fired.

He missed the men, but hit the white man's horse.

Chaco spun his mount, hooked Teacher's elbow, and swung him up into the saddle behind, and in two leaps of his powerful mount, had disappeared up the canyon behind the passengers and their guards.

Ryan, the nearest to the kin's horses, ran for them, but they were at least a hundred fifty yards from his spot in a pile of boulders, and he had to drop down to the road, down the canyon to the cleft, and up its steep bottom to where they'd hidden them.

His three kin were well behind him when he saw the two Indians, whom they'd let pass unmolested, pounding back up the trail toward him. He waved the kin off the road into the rocks. The Indians were less than a hundred yards away when Ryan dropped behind a rock and leveled his Winchester on the lead rider.

He patiently let them get only forty yards away. Then

his Winchester spit fire and he knocked the first Indian out of the saddle, and swung his rifle to the second one, but that man had spun his horse and dropped off the saddle to the side, out of sight of the man with the rifle.

Ryan, unwilling to shoot down the horse, let the man gallop away. He rose from his rest behind the rock, just as Ethan and Dillon ran up. Killian limped along far behind.

"Wait there and watch the trail," Ryan yelled at Killian, then spun on his heel and headed up the cut after the horses.

Again, they heard the pounding of hoofbeats, and all dropped to a knee and brought their rifles to their shoulders.

It was Kane, riding hell-bent-for-leather. He set the buckskin back on its haunches as he slid to a stop alongside Killian.

"What the hell happened?" he asked. "Where are the women?"

Before Kill could answer, Dillon pointed back up the trail. "There's a side cut going east back a couple of hundred yards. Sixdog sent the women up there with a couple of guards, then followed when shooting came from down the trail a ways." He didn't bother to mention that young Ethan had fired too soon.

Kane, to their surprise, fished the revolver smoothly out of the holster on his hip, and fired, shooting between his kin, who jumped aside. They looked behind them to see the Indian Ryan had shot out of the saddle, falling to his back in the dust, his rifle spinning away, a hole neatly in his forehead, and the back of his head blown away. This time Dillon strode over and kicked the man's rifle away, and stooped to jerk an old Navy Colt from where it was stuffed in his belt—only then realizing that the Indian had a crippled arm.

Kane merely spun the buckskin and gave him his heels.

"Damn good shot," Ryan managed.

The rest merely stared, surprised at themselves that they hadn't bothered to fetch the Indian's weapons, even though he'd looked as dead and gone as yesterday.

Morris Flannigan could hear the shots in the distance, echoing back down the trail from the direction Gratsworth had ridden toward.

"Damn him, what did he do now?" Flannigan muttered, walking down off the porch and standing, puffing his pipe like one of his employer's steam engines, watching the trail.

By the time he knocked the dottle out of his pipe, he looked back up to see Gratsworth's horse pounding back down the trail, riderless.

The animal had stepped on his reins and broken them, and the tails hung useless from the bridle. The horse trotted up to the trough that served both the inside and outside of the corral next to the barn.

Morris walked over, and was not surprised to see the horse's mane and neck covered with blood.

"You shot, boy?" he asked. He ran his hands over the horse's neck, and finding no wound, answered his own question. "Nope, it would more'n likely be Collin Gratsworth who's shot. Looks to me by the amount of blood that Cheyenne City's gonna be looking for a new marshal."

He turned to see both of Gratsworth's deputies running toward them. They slid to a stop, wide-eyed, staring at the blood on the horse.

"One of you ride on south and see if you can find Gratsworth. Looks like he ran into trouble."

They studied the horse and the blood, then looked sheepishly and silently at Flannigan.

Finally, Hiram Lavender, the one with his arm still gimpy from Killian's twisting it half off, shook his head as he spoke. "I ain't going up there. I'm still all stove up."

The other one, Marcus McMann, shook his scarred face with equal skepticism. "And I'm a married man, Mr. Flannigan, and my wife's with child. Let's just sit tight a while and see what comes."

Flannigan, wondering what kind of woman would marry a man so ugly and cowardly, and what kind of gargoyle the two of them might bear, stomped away, retook his place in the rocker, and with more vigor than normal, packed his pipe.

Ryan recovered the horses, with Dillon close behind. They rode back down the narrow side canyon, leading Ethan and Killian's animals.

As they mounted, Dillon quickly recounted the situation. "One Indian rode off back toward the stage station, but the bulk of them are with the prisoners. Let's go help Kane." He whipped up his horse, and without argument, the others followed.

Chaco and Teacher had quickly caught up with Spotted-Horse Harry, Badger-Hat, and the hostages. Chaco'd sent Crooked-Arm Charley and Black Eagle on ahead, and had heard all the shots. He would not count on them returning.

"How many you make them?" Chaco asked Teacher. He shrugged. "Only one was shootin', but another four or five raised up out of the rocks. Could be that's all, but could be a damn regiment."

Chaco yelled to Spotted-Horse and Badger-Hat, "In the rocks. Kill whoever follows. Ponies come with us." Then he spurred his horse around the others and took the lead-rope from Spotted-Horse.

"How many?" Spotted-Horse asked him as he dismounted.

Chaco shrugged. "A few, my brother, but they are white men. You will have cover and the high ground. I will hide the women and return."

"Let me go," Venton yelled. "I'll fight with you."

Chaco ignored him, and the women looked at him with newfound hatred.

Spotted-Horse and Badger-Hat knew that Chaco would not think twice about leaving them to die, but said nothing as Chaco gave heels to his horse and, leading the prisoners, clambered into the rocks, leaving their horses in the trail. Teacher leapt from the rump of Chaco's horse, caught the reins of Badger-Hat's game little mare, and before Badger Hat turned to see what had happened, gave heels to the mare and passed the captives to join Chaco in the trail.

Then they pushed their horses as hard as they could, as Spotted-Horse's mount followed, its saddle empty.

Chapter 23

Kane figured he couldn't be more than a quarter mile behind his quarry, and that his kin wouldn't be far behind. Even though his buckskin was well lathered, he pushed the horse hard up into the rocky cleft, its hoofs clattering on the hard shale.

After fifty feet, the chasm flattened and widened to fifty feet. It was mid-morning and the sun was in his face. By the time he was two hundred yards off the road, he caught a glance of the rump of a horse in the distance, and pushed the buckskin into a clambering gallop.

His every nerve ending was afire as he felt the end of his trek near—when he saw a flash on the canyon wall ahead, two hundred yards distant, and the buckskin's forelegs collapsed. He somersaulted over the animal's withers, hitting hard and knocking the wind from his chest. Gasping for breath, he managed to get to his hands and knees, and as two more shots kicked up sand and rock shards in his face, he scrambled for a pile of rocks that would shelter him. Another pair of shots sent chunks flying off the rock he hid behind.

The buckskin tried to get to his feet, blowing foamy lung blood from his nostrils, and from a hole in his chest.

Kane, the taste of bile in his throat, drew the Bland-Pryce, leveled it on the big buckskin's head, and put him out of his misery.

"Sorry, boy," he said, anger replacing the bile and stealing his resolve.

By the time he caught his breath, he heard the beating of hooves behind him. He couldn't let the kin ride under the fire that was coming at him. Taking a deep breath, he got his feet under him, then broke from the rocks, zigging and zagging back down the trail as gunshots rang behind.

He rounded a bend out of sight of the shooters, and came face-to-face with Dillon's pounding horse, having to dive to the side to keep from being overrun.

"Rein up!" he yelled, and Dillon slid to a stop, as did the others following.

"They're in the rocks ahead, at least two of them."

"You hit?" Kill yelled at him.

"No. The buckskin is finished."

"Can we get above them?" Dillon asked, eyeing the canyon walls.

"Easy," Kane said, and began climbing the south wall.

Dillon dismounted, but Ethan beat him off his horse, and was already going up the north wall like a spider on all fours, leaving Kill and Dillon in the trail bottom. Dillon moved forward until he could see up the trail, and pulled his wide-brimmed hat off and waved it. A shot cut the air and ricocheted down the canyon.

"They're a bit touchy," he said to Killian, who still sat his nervous mount.

"Keep them interested until Ethan and Kane can get a bead on them."

"What the hell you think I'm doing," Dillon groused, but waved the hat again. This time two shots rang out, and the hat was holed. Dillon jerked it back and stared at it. "Damn if that will hold water now," he complained, running a finger through the hole.

"Better the hat than your head," Kill said. "Those old boys are fine hands with a rifle. I'm glad we didn't ride out there."

Kane had disappeared up the wall to the south, and Ethan to the north. Dillon waited another couple of minutes, then sailed the hat across the narrow gap. Again, a pair of shots rang out and skipped off the canyon wall near the hat.

"Hell, boys, shoot her full of holes and use up your lead," Dillon said, pulling off his canvas coat. He waited another minute, then waved the coat, attracting another pair of gunshots. Without bothering to try and aim, he pulled his Colt and reached out and fired a couple of rounds up the bottom of the canyon. "That'll keep their interest," he said.

Kane climbed until he found a tree line, then worked his way up the canyon in the shelter of the copse until he thought he was even with where the shooters hid. He caught a glance of Ethan, a couple of hundred yards across the chasm, as he too worked his way up. When he thought he was near a spot where he could drop down and get a shot, he searched for Ethan, but caught no sight of him.

He moved down, out of the trees, hearing shots from the men below, both somewhere below him, and from his kin down the canyon.

The shoulders of the canyon were slick sandstone, and it was hard to keep his footing and watch for the shooters below. It wouldn't do to get to sliding while trying to exchange shots with a man with a rifle.

Straining to see, he caught the flash of movement in the rocks across the canyon, and made out a man in the shadows . . . a man with a fur hat. He was a hundred yards away, too far for a decent shot with the Bland-Pryce. *Damn, I should have borrowed a rifle from one of the boys,* he thought. Both his Winchester and the Springfield were still in the scabbards on the buckskin.

Then he saw Ethan emerge from the tree line above the Indian and begin to work his way down the rock face. He watched as Ethan kicked some rocks loose, which tumbled, then launched into the air, striking the canyon bottom with sounds as sharp and loud as rifle shots. The Indian across the canyon bottom looked up, studying the rock face above, realizing that he was being stalked.

He rearranged himself so he was shielded by a boulder from the edge above, as Ethan worked his way down. He was less than a hundred feet above the man, when Kane decided to act.

He jumped, landing on his butt, and sliding down the slick sandstone surface, trying to level the Bland-Pryce as he slid. On the other side, Ethan found a narrow cleft, and he too bounced from rock to rock, rapidly descending.

Realizing that the Indian knew Ethan was descending, and as the man rounded the boulder to face the new threat with cover, Kane fired, sending shards flying from the boulder, but doing no real harm as the Indian dove aside.

With two shots gone, still sliding, Kane almost dropped on top of another Indian on his side of the cleft, who held a Winchester in hand. Kane was able to kick him as he dropped, knocking the rifle to one side, but

Kane landed hard, losing his balance and going down on his right shoulder.

The Indian spun onto his back, got to one knee, and leveled the Winchester at Kane before he could recover. As Kane was bringing up the Bland-Pryce, the Indian, a triumphant smile on his face, pulled the trigger—then realized he hadn't worked a shell into the chamber after his last shot. Even before Kane could fire, the man was blown spinning aside. He collapsed against the rock wall, staring down, blood blossoming from his chest, and Kane silently thanked Ethan across the now-narrow cleft. The man tried to raise the rifle, but Kane finally got off a shot, and the big .577 bullet, hitting him high in the chest, blew the man sideways to the ground, and the rifle spun aside.

Kane leapt up, seeing that Ethan was also falling directly on top of the Indian with the fur hat. The Indian's attention had been on Kane, but he spun to take Ethan's plunge. He swung the rifle at Ethan, catching him a clipping blow across the head, but Ethan's plunge took him into the man, who let the rifle fall, caught Ethan by the shirtfront, and rolled backward. His feet taking Ethan in the belly, he flipped him over with his backward somersault, sending him flying on down the rock face.

As the Indian hustled for his rifle, Kane recovered the dead Indian's brass-studded Winchester. He levered in a shell and as the Indian jumped atop a small ledge, looking down to find the man who'd fallen on him, Kane fired.

The man dropped his rifle, spinning away down the rock face to where Ethan had recovered his feet and turned to face the threat. The Indian grasped his belly with both hands, doubled, and it was *his* turn to somersault down the rock face to rest at Ethan's feet.

Ethan kicked him aside, then fanned his revolver, firing repeatedly into the man's chest.

The canyon smelled of gunpowder as the smoke cleared.

Kane slid to the canyon bottom and walked over and extended his hand to Ethan. "Good to have you in Wyoming," Kane said, a tight smile on his face.

"Good to have a cousin who can shoot," Ethan said, laughing.

"I'd as soon be lucky as good, and we were damn lucky. Wave the kin on up," Kane said.

In moments, Dillon and Kill were at their side. Dillon carried Kane's Winchester and Springfield across the saddle in front of him, still in their saddle scabbards.

"I need your horse," Kane said to his brother, Kill.

"You'll leave me afoot," Kill complained.

"You're the least able, boyo. You can make your way down to the road, and one of us, or the stage, will be along."

"God damn," Kill complained, dismounting. "It don't pay to get lamed up around this bunch."

"Don't complain," Dillon said as Kane mounted Kill's grulla. Dillon threw Kane his long guns, then a couple of boxes of shells, and Kane strapped them on the saddle and dropped the shells in the saddlebags as Dillon spoke. "You'll be out of it, and it's gonna get worse."

"I don't damn well want out of it," Kill yelled at his three kin as they spun and pounded away up the canyon.

Still mumbling through hard-clamped jaws, his freckled face red, dragging a leg, he limped away back toward the road.

"How far ahead you figure they are?" Dillon yelled at Kane.

"A quarter mile, maybe more. They can't stay ahead, dragging the women."

They hunkered down in the saddle, and concentrated on closing the distance.

Doyle Venton yelled ahead to Chaco, "Cut me loose, give me a gun, and I'll stop those bloody Irishmen."

Chaco reined up, and considered the man's insistent request. He had caused no trouble, had kept to himself, and his few comments had always been of hate for the men who pursued them, and especially for those he owed lead. Chaco had no idea if the man was worth anything as ransom, so maybe it was worth the risk.

He'd heard the shots in the canyon behind, as they'd echoed up, ringing over the sound of the horses' hooves. He knew he might never see Spotted-Horse and Badger-Hat again, as he'd left them no riding stock, forcing them to face the oncoming men, unless they hid out and let the white men pass. And it would not be like either of them to hide from an enemy.

When Chaco topped the canyon to a flat ridge, peppered with lodgepole pine, he reined up, dropped out of the saddle, and walked back. He untied the old piebald's reins, took out his big knife, and cut Venton's bindings. He was tired of leading the women, so he gave Venton a choice. "You lead women, white man. No gun. Prove your worth."

"Fine," Venton said, and spurred the piebald up and gathered up the lead-rope.

"You don't deserve to be called a white man," Viv snapped at him, but he ignored her.

This time, Chaco dropped to the rear of the pack, letting Teacher lead, and Venton follow with the women.

He wanted to keep an eye on the white man, now freed of his bindings. He didn't trust him, but hoped he might be of use.

Teacher led them back down another canyon, heading for the place they'd camped the night before, a narrow cleft with a hard rock trail where an unwary pursuer might lose their trail. He'd have to cross the road, but that was of little worry, as his pursuers were behind him.

Chapter 24

Killion McCreed limped back to the road, cursing under his breath all the way.

When he moved out of the cleft onto the road, he looked back down toward the Greybull Station, wondering if there was any chance he could walk all the way, figuring it must be three or four miles. He knew the stage was due today, but couldn't remember if it was the northbound or the southbound. The southbound would do him no good, as they'd never turn around, in fact, couldn't without moving more than two miles up the canyon.

He decided to give walking a try, even though he knew it would probably set back his recovery.

Only walking a couple of hundred yards, he rounded a small curve, and smiled.

By God, he thought, *I'm not out of it yet.*

The Indian that Dillon had shot coming back up the trail from Greybull, and that Kane had finished off, lay in the road, his pony bending over him.

The little paint stood patiently as Kill limped up and gathered up his rope reins.

Kill looked down at the dead man. "You may be a

dead Indian now, but you were a fair horse trainer. I hope there are horses wherever you're bound, red man."

He led the horse over to a small boulder, mounted it, and managed to settle into the saddle.

Sitting a moment, contemplating the situation, he decided that Chaco's main camp was to the west, and even though they'd lit a shuck to the east up that little side canyon, they would probably circle and head back to the country they knew well. It was just a hunch, but he decided to stay in the road. Besides, his knee hurt too damn much to fight through rocks and brush, ducking tree limbs, and the saddle was uncomfortable to ride. He'd stay in the road, and hope the fight circled back to him.

He set out south on the road, the way the Indians had come.

Kane was close enough to see dust rising above the trees ahead as they dropped back down to the southwest. The trees had thinned as they'd crested the ridge and begun to descend the south slope, and he set the grulla into a gallop. Dillon and Ethan were close behind. He caught the first glance of a rider ahead just as he dropped into a steep cleft, which Kane presumed dropped back down to the stage road. They were making a circle, heading back west.

He reined back and waved his kin up alongside. "Chaco is a rotten no-good, and would as soon shoot the women as not, if he thinks he's not going to get the ransom. We can't just ride in shooting, 'cause one of them's bound to get caught in the gunfire."

"So, what do you want to do?" Dillon shouted over the hoofbeats.

"I'm gonna try and get ahead of them—out on a point where I can see the mouth of that ravine—with the Springfield, and see if I can pick them off."

"We'll keep pressing them, but won't close."

Kane nodded in agreement, and hit the grulla hard with his heels. The horse leapt forward, and they pounded away through the sparse trees.

In less than a half mile, the ridge began to drop away, then fell steeply.

Kane reined the big grulla to a sliding stop, jerked the Springfield from its scabbard, and leapt from the saddle. He had to calm the horse before he could dig in the saddlebags. Ripping the box of shells from the bags, he filled his pockets with shells, then ran south, hoping, praying, that he would be in time.

He reached the edge of a rimrock, and to his dismay, the riders, now six strong, were just riding down out of the ravine onto the road, over four hundred yards away and almost two hundred feet below where he'd taken a position. He fell to a prone position, raised and adjusted the sights, cocked the big rifle, and waited. They'd lined up, going away, and he couldn't shoot at the rear rider, who he made to be the bearded white man, without fear of hitting one of the riders ahead.

He backhanded the sweat out of his eyes, the sun now high overhead, and waited.

Every second meant a longer shot, but the stage road took a hard turn to the right ahead of them, and that might, just might, give him a shot.

Again, he adjusted the sights—five hundred yards.

He steadied his breathing, watching as the lead rider, Chaco, he figured, made the turn, followed by the women.

The old man in the rear had dropped twenty feet or more behind the others—the safest shot.

Kane held his breath, leading the man by fifteen feet as they were moving at an easy lope, and squeezed off a round; the recoil kicked against his shoulder, and black powder billowed from the muzzle.

It seemed an eternity until the bullet kicked up a plume of dirt, below and just in front of the rider. His horse spooked, spinning, and putting him even farther behind the others. As soon as Kane saw the location of the impact, he threw open the breech, pried out the casing, and slammed home another round.

He gave it a little more elevation, and not quite so much lead, held his breath, and pulled off the second with a gentle squeeze.

The man's horse folded out from under him, but the old man lit on his feet in a run, catching up with the last of the women.

Chaco had been searching the skyline to the south as he pounded forward, and saw the muzzle blast of the second shot, far away. He figured the shooter had no chance, until he heard Teacher cry out.

"I'm hit! I'm hit!"

He reined up, but only momentarily, to see Teacher running forward, holding his thigh. His horse was down, so the shot must have gone clean through the leg and killed the animal, although the horse was kicking, trying to regain his feet.

Teacher, now half-dragging his leg, caught up with the fat woman, and jerked her flying out of the saddle.

Chaco drew his revolver and gigged his horse back to face Teacher, who was now mounted.

"You walk," he commanded. "Woman worth gold."

"What?" Teacher said, his jaw dropping.

202 L. J. Martin

"Walk." He turned to Angie Bolander, who lay on the ground, glaring up at them. "Get in saddle."

Teacher's eyes turned hard, and as Chaco's eyes shifted to the woman, he reached for his revolver. It didn't clear the holster before Chaco fired, blowing him back, and fired again before he hit the ground.

Then he swung his muzzle to Angie. "Back in saddle."

There was no question in her mind that Chaco would shoot her where she lay, and even though exhausted from the hard ride, she quickly rose and remounted.

Chaco turned to Doyle Venton. "You get his share, you fight with me?"

Venton nodded his head in agreement.

"Get his guns and follow," Chaco commanded, riding forward and taking the lead-rope from Venton, who dropped back. Chaco gave heels to the horse just as Angie settled in the saddle.

Vivian shouted at him, "Why don't you ride on, escape, and leave us behind?" But he didn't turn, nor answer, just pulled the horses on down the road.

Kane watched all this transpire, unable to shoot because they were gathered close together.

He looked down below, and saw Dillon and Ethan gallop out of the cleft, and at the same time, his younger brother, Killian, trotted in the road below him on an Indian pony.

"That overgrown whelp's got no quit in him," Kane muttered to himself, and he ran back and forked the grulla again, then spurred the big horse directly ahead, into a steep slope that he had no idea if either of them could survive.

After two leaps, the big horse locked his front legs and set back, his rump dragging the ground, as they slid down the hill, starting small landslides in their path. Halfway, the grulla slipped to his side and rolled, and Kane was barely able to jump clear as the horse tumbled but then regained his footing as Kane caught up, grabbed up his reins, and dragged the horse behind him, slipping and sliding to the stage road. Again, he mounted, and they pounded after the kin, who were almost to where Teacher had been shot from his horse.

They waited for Kane to catch up, staring down at the old man, who was still breathing.

"They musta had a disagreement," Dillon said, a wry smile on his face.

Kane caught up, leapt from his saddle, and pulled Kill's canteen out of his saddlebag. He crossed to the old man, and poured water in his face.

His eyes opened, and his gaze went from man to man.

"He left you to die," Kane said.

"He . . . he caused me to die," Teacher said, half his mouth turned up in a smile.

"You don't owe him the sweat off your brow," Kane said.

"I . . . I don't owe a living soul," Teacher said, "but I wouldn't mind owing one of y'all a slug of whiskey . . . I'm fresh out."

"We got no whiskey."

"Hell of a note, going to hell with no whiskey in your gullet."

"True, it's a hell of a note. Where's Chaco going?" Kane asked him.

Teacher spit blood onto the ground beside him, and shrugged one shoulder. "He . . . he doesn't seek my . . . my counsel," the old man said, his voice growing weaker. "Just leave me die in peace," Teacher said, again closing his eyes.

Kane shrugged, replaced the canteen, and swung back up in the saddle, then kicked the grulla into a gallop, leaving the others staring after him.

"He don't talk much," Dillon said to Kill.

"Too damn much for me at times," Kill said, and gave his heels to the Indian pony, following, as the rest joined up behind, leaving the badly bleeding old man to his own troubles.

Within minutes, Kane had Chaco and the others in sight. He watched as they turned off the trail to the west, to the cleft near where he'd climbed the cliff. This time, he was hot after them, with the kin only a hundred yards behind.

The arroyo was steep-sided, too steep for a horse, and the walls led up to vertical rim rocks. As they neared the top of the cut, Chaco reined aside, handed the lead-rope to Vivian, and snarled an order. "Keep going."

When Venton drew even, Chaco had his revolver trained on his midsection. He snapped at Venton, "You get in rocks and kill them as they come."

"I don't even know how many cartridges in this Winchester and Colt," Venton complained.

"Then make bullets count," Chaco said, his weapon cocked and ready for trouble from this man he barely knew.

Venton jumped from the piebald, and led him to a nearby pine and tied him, then ran back down the cut to where he could hide in the rocks.

Chaco rode away behind the women.

Venton had barely settled in, when he saw oncoming riders. He fired at the lead man.

Kane felt a bullet cut through his shirt, burning his side, and he dove from the horse. Behind him, the kin scattered into the rocks.

By the time he raised up from behind a rock, he saw Venton's back disappearing as he ran for his horse. He didn't bother to fire at the man, who was over 150 yards away, dodging in and out of the rocks, as Kane decided then and there that he wanted to be looking into his eyes when he killed him.

Kane searched the rocks, wondering if Sixdog was hiding there, waiting to shoot them out of the saddle, but not seeing him, ran for the grulla and mounted again, and again gave heels to the horse.

This time, he meant to ride Sixdog to ground.

Hell or high water, Sixdog was going to meet his Maker.

Chapter 25

Venton caught up the piebald, and rather than go after Sixdog and the women, he moved off the trail at the top of the cut and rode into the trees on the step where Kane had rested the night before.

Kane got to where he'd seen Venton leave the trail, and saw only one set of hoofprints going that way. He stayed in the main drainage, figuring that Sixdog and the women were up ahead, heading for where they'd holed up the night before.

In moments, Kane topped the cut and set the grulla into a gallop across the flat, through the trees, that ended in the place where Chaco had camped.

Chaco passed the women, but didn't bother to grab the lead-rope away from Vivian, who was using it as a makeshift rein. Instead, he yelled at her, "Keep going, up through trees." Then he jumped from the saddle just below the campsite, its fire still smoking from the night before. Dragging his Winchester with him, he took cover in a tight copse of lodgepole, where he could see his back trail for fifty yards.

He watched Vivian, as she followed his instructions,

riding clumsily and slowly with the little girl still in front of her, and the other two horses tied on behind. As soon as they passed into the trees out of the clearing that had served as campsite, and out of Sixdog's sight, Angie Bolander threw a leg over the saddle and jumped from the moving horse. She recovered her feet, gathered her skirt in hand, and ran into the woods. Marybeth Pettersen saw what she'd done, and followed suit, leaping, gathering up her skirts, and running into the woods on the other side of the game trail, the opposite direction from Angie.

Doyle Venton had circled the camp, and gotten behind them. He watched through the trees as Chaco sent the women on ahead, right into his waiting arms. Then he was surprised when, before they reached where he hid in the shadows, two of the women made a break for it, going in opposite directions, while the blond with the cropped hair and the child in front of her kept coming.

Kane was at a hard gallop, when he felt the slap of a bullet past his face. He dropped low in the saddle, and kept moving; then another bullet hit him and knocked him out of the saddle. He rolled and scrambled into the brush as the grulla pounded on. He drew his Bland-Pryce as soon as he stopped rolling.

As soon as he was hidden from view, he felt for the wound, and found that a bullet had struck his thick leather belt, gouged through it, and taken a finger-sized track of flesh out of his side and back, but had left him little harmed. It burned like hell, and was gushing blood, but he'd live.

He scrambled forward toward where he thought the bullet had come from in the trees ahead.

The others rode up behind him, and he heard another shot, then the kin yelling and scrambling for cover.

He moved forward quickly from tree to tree.

Another shot splattered the bark over his head, and he dropped to the ground. It had come from not more than twenty paces in front of him.

He yelled out, "Give it up, Sixdog."

"I know voice," Sixdog said quizzically.

"It's Kane McCreed. I've come to take you in."

Sixdog laughed, then with derision said, "You come to join your friend, who Chaco killed in Deer Lodge, as I kill you now."

"Throw down your weapons, and you'll live to hang . . . but you'll live," Kane shouted, and lied. He meant to kill Chaco Sixdog, who had killed two of his friends . . . the first in Deer Lodge prison; the second, Vivian Flynn's husband.

He meant to bring his head to Morris Flannigan.

"Ride away, or I kill woman and child," Chaco said.

"Vivian!" Kane shouted, wondering where she was, hoping he'd get a feeling for her location, so he wouldn't shoot in that direction.

He got no answer, but heard Sixdog moving away at a run, breaking brush.

Kane listened carefully, trying to judge where Sixdog was now, and where Vivian and the other women might be.

He heard brush breaking behind him, and spun to see Dillon on his hands and knees, coming to join him.

"Where is he?" Dillon asked.

"He was right in front of me, not more than twenty paces, but he moved away. I couldn't fire as I didn't know where the women were."

"Kill is circling to the north and Ethan to the south. We'll have him boxed in."

Just then, from three or four hundred yards away, a

long spine-racking scream echoed down out of the trees above the camp, stopping Kane cold. It was Vivian.

He broke into a run.

"I'll bring the horses!" Dillon called from behind.

Doyle Venton charged out of the thicket on the piebald. He wanted one of the horses Vivian still led, and her, as she was worth money to the railroad. He figured he still might salvage something of this circus. He rode right into Vivian, grabbing for her, wanting to drag her out of the saddle, but he got his hands on little Cassie instead, and wrenched her out of Vivian's hands.

The little girl was screaming at the top of her lungs, but Venton quickly decided she was worth even more than the woman. Vivian, still astride and beside him, flailed at him, screaming at the top of her lungs. Venton hit her hard with his fist, knocking her out of the saddle. He snatched up the lead-rope to the two horses following, spun the piebald, and set off into the trees away from the campsite and the gunfire below, leaving the woman, figuring the child to be much less trouble. Vivian's horse trotted along behind, dragging his single lead-rope.

Venton figured he'd ride well away, change horses, then head for Greybull, where he'd trade the little girl for either some ransom money or reward money—he cared not which.

Vivian was knocked senseless, but every gram of her being said, "Save Cassie." She struggled to her feet, bleeding from an ear, her head swimming.

She heard crashing behind her, and prayed it was Kane McCreed, whom she'd seen in the canyon when the chase first began.

She struggled to her feet, then screamed again, as Chaco Sixdog galloped out of the brush. She spun and had only made a couple of strides, when he swept her up in the saddle in front of him, draping her across the horse, and the animal charged forward. In moments they were out of the trees and on a rocky slope leading up. Then Chaco jerked rein, dragged her upright, and forced her leg over the horse's head. She began to scream again, then felt Chaco's big blade pressing into her throat. Cold fear silenced her.

He whispered in her ear. "I leave your head here, you yell again. Understand?"

She tried to nod her head, but the blade was pressed so deeply into her throat that she could barely move. Chaco apparently accepted the slight movement, and removed the blade, re-sheathing it, and gave his heels to the horse, which leapt forward up the rocky escarpment.

He glanced back to see Kane McCreed break out of the brush at the toe of the slope, and laughed, as he was afoot and would never catch up.

Black Eagle had ridden hard to escape the ambush, and the men who'd shot Crooked-Arm Charley out of the saddle. He'd circled west off the road, and was over a mile above the canyon, high in the ponderosas at the snow line, when he'd heard the shooting in the canyon below, and figured that Chaco and the rest of them had ridden into the ambush.

The shooting had gone on for a while, as he'd ridden south across the face of the mountain. He'd intended to return to where they'd camped the night before, as Chaco had instructed them to meet up there, should the ransom of the captives not go well—and it hadn't.

After a few miles of riding in the high lonely, he was working his way down toward that camp, when he again heard gunfire below. Apparently, whoever the ambushers were, they had chased his comrades all the way back to the campsite.

He spurred his horse forward, thinking he might get a high position to fire down on the fight, when he heard the wailing of a child. Reining up, he waited in silence, then realized the wailing was coming closer. He sprang from the saddle, taking his Winchester, and moved along a rimrock, then stopped and waited again.

A voice rang out. "Stop that caterwaulin', or I'll knock you on the head." But the crying didn't stop.

Black Eagle could see the bobbing of a hat, then a face; then a man on horseback appeared out of the brush, with the child in the saddle in front of him. It was the man they'd captured, riding with the child of the man and woman they'd killed.

They rode on a game trail just below the small rimrock where he hunkered in the brush.

Letting them get even with him, he drew his knife, then leapt, taking the man out of the saddle, one arm around his neck. They hit hard, but not so hard that Black Eagle could not bring his other hand and the knife across the white man's throat.

The white man gurgled, his head fell to the side, and blood gushed from his slit throat, as he tried to quell the bleeding with both hands. The white man had dragged the little girl off with him, and blood spurted over her now-soiled-and-torn yellow dress. She suddenly stopped crying, and clambered to her feet, staring at the dead man at her feet, as Black Eagle too gained his feet.

The white man lay unmoving, his eyes open, but vacant.

Black Eagle glared at the little girl, then swept her up in his arms, and clambered up the rock face to recover his black gelding.

Chaco pushed the little now-burdened horse hard up the rocks. High above he could see the tree line, where snow began.

To his surprise, a white man, well above them on the slope, rode an Indian pony. They saw each other at the same time, and the white man jumped from his horse, taking a rifle with him, and clambered into the rocks.

Chaco spun the horse, and retraced his steps.

Kill, riding the Indian paint, had circled the camp, high above where he'd have the best view of the country, and it had paid off. But he was surprised to see the Indian with one of the women in the saddle in front of him. He considered trying to kill the horse, but it was too great a risk. Instead, he ran to recover the pony, mounted, and followed.

Kane, hoping for a shot, praying that Vivian would free herself and leap from the saddle, praying that something would happen so he could end this, gave chase on foot. He was almost as fast as a horse, going up the escarpment.

To his shock, he was suddenly face-to-face with Vivian, with Chaco's ugly face over her shoulder.

The instant she saw Kane, she turned and lay back, raking her nails over Chaco's already scarred face.

He grunted and slapped her aside, knocking her out of the saddle.

Kane raised the Bland-Pryce, but he was too close as Chaco had dug his heels into the paint's side and was clawing for his own revolver, stuffed into his sash belt. The paint tried to avoid running over Kane, and veered to the side, but Chaco managed to kick out with a moccasined foot, and knocked Kane flying.

The big Indian threw himself off the horse, lit, spun, and was after Kane, who was flat on his back.

Chaco dove for him, as he was raising the heavy pistol.

They locked wrists, Chaco with his left hand grabbing Kane's revolver arm, and Kane grabbing Chaco's. They rolled, down the steep escarpment, bouncing from boulder to boulder, still locked together, knowing the first one to lose his grip would die.

Shoving and wrenching, they managed to get to their feet, and Chaco fell back, flipping Kane over his head, but each clung to the other's wrist and they came up together.

Kane, having grown up with the kin, cousins and brothers, was well schooled in rough-and-tumble wrestling, and Chaco had spent his youth pinning every brave in his tribe. Chaco again started to fall back, but only feinted and stepped forward, getting a foot behind Kane's ankle, and they again went to the ground, rolling.

But this time Kane came up on top. Slightly shorter than Chaco, he crashed his head down, three times hard, headbutting the Indian on the bridge of his nose. Blood spurted, but Chaco managed to roll, taking Kane with him.

They dropped over a six-foot ledge and hit hard, this time with Kane on the bottom. It knocked the breath from Kane, and he let Chaco's wrist go free.

Chaco stumbled back, but collected himself and rose to full height, his revolver in hand. Kane got to his feet. Chaco leveled in on Kane's chest, as he straightened up.

Chaco gave him a hard smile that crossed his wide, scarred face. "It time you join your fri—"

Chapter 26

But Chaco Sixdog didn't finish the sentence.

Kane thought he was dead, that Chaco had fired, but the shot came from behind him, from over his shoulder, from up atop the ledge.

Chaco stumbled backward, his revolver falling aside. Kane heard the lever action of a rifle, and another shot roared in his ears as he spun to see Vivian, holding a brass-studded Winchester she'd pulled from Chaco's saddle.

He turned back to see Chaco, leaning against a rock face, staring down at two holes in his chest, each pumping blood. He dropped to his knees, then fell on his face, unmoving.

Kane turned back to Viv, then climbed up as she cast the rifle aside and fell into his arms. Then she pushed away. "That Venton man has Cassie, and Marybeth and Angie ran into the woods, somewhere down below."

Before she finished the sentence, Kill rode down from above and jumped from the saddle, and below them, Ethan and Dillon were pushing their horses up the escarpment, leading the grulla.

They gathered together. Dillon was smiling, and asked, "We taking him down the mountain?"

"Not quite yet," Kane said. "We've got two other women, who ran off in the woods. You and Ethan go fetch them back, and Kill and I will go after the little girl. Viv says Doyle Venton rode off with her."

Dillon and Ethan both mounted up, and Kane headed for the grulla, when Viv cried out, "Look!"

All of them looked where she was pointing. Fifty yards above them, on the edge of a rock outcropping, Black Eagle sat his horse, Cassie in front of him on the saddle, leaning back, her eyes seeming to be closed.

She was covered with blood.

"My, God," Viv said, "he's killed her." She collapsed to her knees, bringing her hands to her face and sobbing.

But Kane watched as Black Eagle grabbed the little girl and lifted her out of the saddle. She looked up at him and smiled as he lowered her to the ground. He looked around and, seeing those below, waved.

Black Eagle spun his horse and was gone.

"I'll get her," Kill said, his freckled face carrying a wide grin as he gigged his horse up the mountain.

"Look, Viv, look," Kane said. "She's laughing and smiling."

"What?" Viv said with a sob, dropping her hands away. "She's laugh—" She quickly stood, then shouted, "Cassie, stay right there! Killian's coming."

In minutes, Cassie was back in her arms.

They loaded Chaco's body, tying it across his horse, and headed down the mountain.

Morris Flannigan was still sitting in one of the rocking chairs, smoking his pipe, when they rode up. Beside him filling the other rocker was Olaf Pettersen, on his feet for the first time as Martha Pettibone had insisted he stay flat on his back for a while, only letting him up to use the thunder pot.

Kane led, trailing Chaco's horse with Chaco's body draped across it, with Vivian behind with Cassie again in the saddle in front of her. Behind her rode Angie Bolander, then Marybeth Pettersen. And behind them, Dillon and Ethan McCabe with Ryan O'Rourke leading a horse with the body of Cheyenne's marshal, Collin Gratsworth, draped across it.

Kane reined up at the hitching rail, dismounted, beat the dust off his trousers, ran a splayed-fingered hand through his unruly dark-red hair, then walked up to stand in front of Morris Flannigan, who was taking it all in.

"Looks like you been busy," Flannigan said.

"You don't mind if his head is still attached to his body. I brought you Chaco's head."

"I called you off. We put the word out we would pay for the captives, and then let the Army handle Sixdog."

Dillon mounted the stairs, escorting Marybeth Pettersen, and Olaf interrupted the exchange by struggling to his feet. "Marybeth. I come to fetch you home."

"I ain't going home, Olaf. I'm going to California. You go on home now. Nobody asked you to come find me."

The big man stared at her in silence, as Kane took the opportunity to continue.

"Flannigan, you're trying to tell me there's no reward—"

"Like hell," Dillon snapped, fishing into his shirt pocket and pulling out a folded paper. He unfolded it and threw it down in Flannigan's lap. "This here's a poster, issued by your railroad, saying you'll pay ten thousand dollars for Chaco Sixdog."

Flannigan stared at the paper, then up at Dillon. "Too late. We rescinded the offer."

Dillon glanced down at the leather saddlebag at the side of Flannigan's rocker. "That the ransom money?" he asked.

Flannigan reddened, then muttered, "That's railroad property."

Dillon reached down and snatched up the saddlebag and dug into it, coming up with a handful of gold coins. He turned to his brother Ethan. "Ethan, lad, you was always good with a pencil. How about you go inside to Mrs. Pettibone's table and count out ten thousand in reward money."

"You can't—" Flannigan said, and tried to stand, but Kane pushed him back down in the rocker.

"I'd suggest you sit there and rock and count your blessings, or take your penknife and go ahead and saw old Chaco's head off, if that's the only part of him you want."

"The hell—" Flannigan complained again.

"There's ladies present, Morris. Where's your manners? A contract is a contract, and possession is nine tenths of the law. We'll just possess the reward and see if you want to go find a judge who says it's yours or ours."

Flannigan sighed deeply, thinking he was beaten, when a new voice rang out. "I think not!"

Deputy Marcus McMann, holding a cocked Winchester, stood in the road next to Deputy Hiram Lavender, also holding a rifle. The rifles were leveled on Kane and Dillon.

Kane and Dillon, hands resting on the butts of their revolvers, eased apart on the porch, and Kill, still mounted and behind Angie Bolander, dropped from the saddle, taking his rifle with him. Ryan O'Rourke merely eased his revolver from the holster, and laid it across the saddle, spinning his mount to face the two deputies.

Kill McCreed also walked back out on the porch, carrying Olaf Pettersen's double barrel Greener.

Kane looked from man to man, then back at the deputies. "So far, all you two got out of the kin is a twisted arm. You want to try for carrying a pound of lead each, courtesy of the McCreeds, the McCabes, and Mr. O'Rourke there, who has no love lost for law officers?"

"We got the drop on you," McMann said nervously.

"Let me see . . . you got the drop on Dillon and me, but Ethan there has a double barrel scattergun ready to spread your guts all over the road, and Ryan and Kill over there both have palmed weapons." Kane laughed and shook his head. "Were I two city deputy dudes, I'd worry about getting saddled up and getting my dead marshal back home where some good souls who didn't know him too well might want to read over him—give him a decent Christian burial."

McMann looked to Flannigan. "Mr. Flannigan?"

Morris shook his head, and gave them a tight smile. "Cheyenne's already got one man to bury. I don't think they'd appreciate having to cough up the dough for two more coffins."

McMann and Lavender both slowly lowered their rifles; then McMann shrugged and asked Flannigan, "Should we saddle up?"

"Yep, and saddle up mine too. We'll be riding out, soon as that young'n in there brings me the railroad's change."

Angie dismounted and ambled up on the porch, holding

her back with one hand. "I'm sore as a boil from a month in the saddle, but I'm hungry as a she-bear fresh from hibernation for some real cooking."

Morris Flannigan rose and stretched. "If you ladies can cook, Mrs. Pettibone is out hunting with her husband, and I don't expect them back till nightfall."

"We can cook," they all three said in unison, and disappeared inside.

Flannigan slapped Kane on the back, then brushed his hands as the dust billowed. "Good job, if a mite expensive."

"That means," Kane said, "that we'll be square."

"Don't forget to tell that lad to only count out ninety-five hundred. You owe for the advance. You want a cigar? This time it's on me."

"Don't mind if I do, but it'll be five cigars, not one. I got kin."

Morris Flannigan and the deputies had ridden out after the women had prepared a big meal and they'd all eaten.

It was dusk, with a golden sunset turning orange over the mountains to the west, when Vivian Flynn walked out on the porch, where the men were enjoying their cigars.

Kane looked up and smiled. Even with her hair cropped short, with the lantern light of the stage station behind her, Viv was a beautiful woman.

He rose from his rocking chair, and the other men followed suit.

"Don't stand," she said, and they all sat back down. "I'm stuffed to the top." She gave all of them a smile, then looked at Kane. "I don't imagine one of you gentlemen would take an evening stroll with me?"

"I will," Kill said quickly.

"No, you won't," Kane corrected with a tone that said he damn well meant it. He grabbed his hat off his head. "I'd be proud to walk with you, Mrs. Flynn."

Dillon, Ethan, and Ryan chuckled at Kill's red face, turning as red as his freckles, as Kane offered Vivian his arm and they walked down the stairs and disappeared into the darkness.

Out beyond the barn, well out of earshot of the others, Viv stopped and turned to face Kane. "Cassie, and I, and the ladies, owe you a great big thank-you."

"You don't owe me anything, Viv. Heck sakes, I was after the reward."

"You know, Kane McCreed, I've known you about as long as any man, and I know when you're lying, and you're lying right now."

He smiled sheepishly. "I never was very good at it." Then he turned serious. "You know, Viv, I've cared about you since before you knew Shamus."

"Cared? Or loved?"

The question caught him short. He'd spent a lot of time thinking about this conversation, and now he was tongue-tied.

"You're not answering?" she queried, a coy smile crossing her beautiful face, now gleaming in the early moonlight.

"I can't, my old hard heart's in my throat."

"You can trust your heart with me, Kane. Shamus loved you like a brother, he'd want . . . he'd want you and me . . ."

Kane thought he saw the glisten of a tear in her eye. Then she smiled, and added, "And to tell the long-lost truth, I'd hoped you'd say something to me long before Shamus came along. I'd given up hoping, but now . . . ."

"But now . . . but now you're coming to Montana with me," he said, grinning, and didn't wait for her answer but gathered her in his arms.

She stopped him short, pushing away. "And Cassie? She's got no kin. And I love her as my own."

"Cow and a calf in the bargain. How could I resist? I got enough carin' to go around."

She shook her head, and laughed. "We'll go to work on how you talk to a lady . . . but that'll come later."

He stifled her laugh, lifting her swinging into the air, then covering her mouth with his.